Winner of an Avery Hopwood Award in poetry at the University of Michigan, the John Day Novel Award at the New School for Social Research for 'Streams in the Wilderness', and author of 'Seek Haven', a volume of verse, Chayym Zeldis has contributed poetry, fiction and criticism to various publications. He spent nine years living on various agricultural settlements in Israel. He is a member of the Poetry Society of America.

D1146606

For Arno Gruen

Chayym Zeldis

Golgotha

Futura Publications Limited
A Contact Book

A Contact Book

First published in Great Britain in 1975
by Futura Publications Limited,
49 Poland St, London W1A 2LG

Copyright © Chayym Zeldis 1974

Published by arrangement with the author

ISBN 0 8600 72037

Printed in Great Britain by
Cox & Wyman Ltd,
London, Reading and Fakenham

Futura Publications Limited
49 Poland Street, London W1A 2LG

PART ONE

ONE

It was a strange Passover supper. There were no women pre-occupied with the food, no children scrambling after the *afikomen*, only Jesus himself and the twelve men seated at the table in the spacious courtyard under a skyful of spring stars. The meal had dragged on for hours, with endless courses and the incessant muttering of prayers. Some of the disciples had gorged themselves and drunk too much of the strong, sweet wine; a few were all but asleep in their places, resting weary heads in their hands and belching softly from indigestion into the heels of their greasy palms.

Jesus himself was wide awake. He had eaten little, touched the wine only in deference to the ritual prescriptions of the Law, and had spoken not at all on his own initiative. He had answered only when addressed by one of the others directly and then as sparingly as possible. Secretly, he was impatient for the ceremony to be done with and the company to disperse. But outwardly, he was relaxed, leaning back on the bench as tradition dictated, his head tilted slightly to one side, the merest suggestion of a smile on his lips, his long fingers toying with scattered bits of *matzah* on the table.

He was depressed. Almost as soon as the meal had begun, an uneasy feeling came over him and increased in severity as the evening progressed. Nothing seemed to relieve it: neither the solemnity of the Passover liturgy and the memories of childhood and the past it evoked; nor the softness of the sky over which the stars lay easily like seashells; nor the gentle gusts of wind that slowly stirred the upper branches of the cypresses lining the road that led into the yard; nor yet the familiar countenances of his comrades and followers who sat with him, as they had so many times before, at ceremonial table.

Jesus found no comfort in any of these things. The sense of solace that he often found in past experience relived in memory – especially in childhood, experience which could be chewed over endlessly like some savoury mash – was gone. He had no idea when, if ever, it would return. For some time now, nature, in which he had always put so much stock and in whose glorious and varied aspects he saw the workings of a cosmic hand, gave him no special sign. There was nothing he could fathom beneath its surface. His friends, his so-called disciples, had seemed for some time to be remote; he felt that it was becoming more and more impossible for him to truly know any one of them, or for them to know him.

He was wide awake, but tonight he had the feeling that he was acting in a dream. He felt that the world and existence itself were dreams. He was dismayed about his feelings, but there was nothing he could do about them.

Toward him a servant came carrying in her hands a carafe of the strong wine he had not tasted. He glanced at her; he had noticed her earlier in the evening. She was young and most certainly a Jerusalemite with dark hair that framed her swarthy face. Her lithe body seemed to have a life of its own as she moved effortlessly, dreamily, with the precision and grace of an animal. The sight of her warmed him suddenly and made him feel better. He wanted to smile openly at her and perhaps even take her by the wrist. He wondered what would happen if he did so. When she came close to him and offered him the wine, he refused. He noticed his refusal mirrored in the eyes of several of the company.

When he saw this, Jesus felt the need to smile and he hid his mouth behind his fingers in a bitter smile tinged with irony that would not have been understood. It seemed to him that everything he did and said lately was misunderstood. The more he lived, the less it seemed possible for him to be understood by others. For a long time he sat motionless in his place, thinking of the servant girl who had offered him the wine. He considered how warm and good her body might be and reflected that he did not know her name. She had moved away and he did not wish to call her back. The cry of a nightingale made him sad; he felt that somehow it was the call of his own dreaming, unsure heart.

TWO

Inside the kitchen, flames leaped up from the great fireplace, casting a red net over the restless figures of the cooks and servants. A reddish pall shone on the greasy stone walls and gleamed in the sweat of faces and limbs in constant motion. The servant girl, whom Jesus had seen and admired, stood without moving in the centre of the room and wiped her brow with her wrist. A look of puzzlement and then of bewilderment came over her fine, regular features, darkened her face, and gave to it a crude, uneven cast.

'Hey, you there, what in the name of God are you standing there and dreaming about?' screamed the chief cook, his perpetual scowl deepening with the effort of making himself heard above the din. He motioned impatiently for the girl to come over to him. She did.

His voice had startled her. He was right, of course. She certainly had been dreaming on her feet. A strange, haunting dream had come from nowhere and overwhelmed her. In it, the sorrowful, isolated man, who was at once the centre of attention at the Passover table in the courtyard and yet somehow seemed not even to be there at all, had come to her in a secluded place. With gentle hands he had removed her garments and put his lips to the nipples of her breasts. He did no other thing to her, did not touch any other part of her body, made no move to embrace her, spoke no word to her. She suffered him to do as it pleased him to do, not daring to touch him in return, not even daring to move from her place. Thus she stood, completely naked, before him and he knelt before her and softly sucked her breasts and then buried his head between them in what to her seemed despair.

Dream was a weak word for what she had imagined. She had seen a vision of erotic power that had fired her senses; yet it went far beyond sensuality and had some meaning quite apart from it. She did not know which of the two of them had been

8

the giver in the dream, or even what was being given. She did know, though, that she had been clothed in her nakedness while he had been naked in his sorrow.

The cook snarled, 'Here, you, take care of this and look sharp about it!' He shoved a large, scorched vessel with lopsided ears at her. The cook was a big, beefy man. As he hurriedly turned again to his fire, his meaty face streaked black with soot and ruddy with firelight, drops of sweat flew from his forehead and splattered the girl. She shivered with fear and estrangement. She bore the vessel across the kitchen, went through a side doorway, and came out into the small yard where the well was located.

Faint illumination from the kitchen fire lay on the swollen buds of the oleander bush on her right. The stars above her wriggled like larvae in their vast cocoon of darkness. To her left was a retaining wall; occasionally a breeze kneaded the whip-like branches of the acacias that ran alongside it. She walked out to the well in the centre of the dusty yard and pulled with trembling fingers at the rope. It was moist and worn with undone strands. The touch of it steadied her somewhat. She breathed more easily in the open air than in the kitchen. Her strong body fell instantly into the rhythm of the work. The pulley creaked. From the surrounding hills, lost in impenetrable shadow, the solitary cry of a jackal drifted down. The sound was high, thin, and fragile; it seemed to shatter as soon as it was uttered and to reach her in fragments. From around the corner of the house, where the Passover service was being concluded, the hushed voices of the celebrants reached her. Again, with frightening clarity, she saw the image of the man at her proffered breasts. The power of the vision caused her to spill the bucket of water she had drawn from the well.

THREE

The hovel was a mean one – low, windowless, and with a roof the wind and rain had gnawed with unrelenting ferocity. It was the very last dwelling in a narrow, dark, garbage-laden cul-de-sac. As she made her way swiftly through the streets of the quarter toward it, the dogs of the poor set up their usual impotent outcry. Once, as she walked with head bent low, a pair of hooded men came out at her from the shadow of an archway, but she whirled on them with unsuspected savagery and threatened them with a knife pulled from her cloak. They quickly left, calling her vile names as they went.

At length, she reached the cul-de-sac and made her way down it. A rat scurried across her path, but she paid no attention to it. She reached her doorway and stood before it without moving for some moments. It apparently took an effort of will for her to enter. She heard the fitful stirrings of the street's animals and far beyond them from the hills, like some gallery of distant relatives, the tenuous, mocking screams of the jackals. They seemed to her the voices of lost and perished souls. From a nearby hovel, an infant cried weakly. If she had hoped in her pause to hear something else, she did not hear it. She bent her head, unfastened the door and entered. She thought the old man would still be up. He was.

A tiny stone oil lamp, burning the crudest of fuels, flickered in the corner. It illuminated only faintly the small area of the room where the old man sat hunched over; he always dozed in that manner, looking like a sackful of rags. Now, as she closed the door behind her, he stirred and cleared his throat loudly; beside him, too old and too lazy to move but also wanting to show her a sign of recognition, the dog lifted its muzzle from the floor. She could hear the breath rattling heavily from its chest. She bolted the door shut and then leaned against it and sighed – heavily, wearily, painfully, as if she could only now allow herself the luxury of letting emotions damned up during the day flow freely.

After a time, she addressed the old man softly. 'Are you up? Did you wait for me to come home?'

She got no answer; indeed, she had not expected one. She went slowly across the room and reached down and touched the old man's shoulder. He did not respond, though she knew he was awake, knew that he had waited for her. He was obdurate, inert, erratic, and often genuinely untrustworthy, and yet he maintained some perverse kind of loyalty to her. The loyalty was the thread by which he managed to cling to life. He and the dog were much alike.

She squatted down beside the old man. His hair was matted with straw and dirt; his cheeks and chin were overrun with grey-white stubble that glistened like fungus in the glow of the lamp. At some time during the evening, he had been gnawing on a chicken bone; its grease shone on his shrunken lips.

'Here,' the girl said, 'this is for you. I brought it from the Passover feast at the master's house.' She drew forth a leg joint of lamb and several flat, platter-like pieces of unleavened Passover bread from a cloth in which she had wrapped them. 'Go ahead, take them, old man.'

He snatched the food from her fingers and, using his several remaining teeth, tore greedily into the meat. He hugged the sheets of bread closely to his chest with his other hand. The dog growled. Its thin voice faded to a high-pitched whine. It was too lazy to stir from its place, or perhaps it was too close to death to really exert itself for a scrap of food. Perhaps, though, death was already feeding it with another kind of food.

The girl sat quietly, yawned, and watched the old man devour the meat ravenously. He slobbered and shook as he ate in the unsteady light of the lamp. In the deeply shadowed opposite corner, her half brother slept on his straw pallet. His choked breath occasionally exploded into snoring. The old man wolfed down his food; he wanted to finish off every scrap of it before the sleeper awoke.

Suddenly, exhaustion overcame the girl. She felt she could not remain awake another moment. She was too weary even to get on her feet, and so she crept on all fours to her own pallet.

Sleep came to her almost as soon as she stretched her body out on the straw, but in the last instant of wakefulness she saw in her mind for the third time that evening the face of the man who had refused the wine offered at the Passover table. The vision shone brilliantly, like a full moon: it was remote, enigmatic, hypnotic. And then a dark cloud of unconsciousness obscured it.

FOUR

The spacious courtyard was finally silent; the clatter from the kitchen and the bustle of servants had died down. The night sky, bit into at its horizons by the hills surrounding Jerusalem, curved luminously overhead, like a great archway beyond which were concealed all of the mysteries of life and death. Under the branches of a fig tree near the gate, an enormous hound snorted fitfully. Just over the wall on the side of the courtyard where the arbour was placed, a jackass brayed once and, as if regretting it, fell quiet.

Jesus started. The animal's voice, breaking over him like a wave, was pure; its starkness and directness seemed to cut through the pretense and hypocrisy of men. He thought of going to the place where the jackass was tethered, but it would have been of no use. Neither he nor the beast would have been able to penetrate the barrier between them. He felt bitter and weary. He wanted very much to sleep – even to sleep forever. He did not feel that something could come from life. He felt old and used up and tired to the point of indifference. What was the use of it all?

He fidgeted on the bench and shifted his weight and inadvertently knocked a flat of Passover bread to the ground. Depressed, he stared at it in the dust. In a sudden fit of bitterness, long repressed, he set his sandal on it and crushed it to bits. He looked around to see if anyone had observed him, and then he was ashamed that he had done so.

A hot, heavy hand with an unrelenting grip touched his shoulder. He knew very well whose hand it was without bothering to look up. Yes, it was the hand of a butcher. Soon the butcher's wine-reeking breath was blowing in his face. He winced, and he fought the urge to lash out with a fist and smash the mug that had dropped low to his cheek and ear. When he felt he had enough control over his voice, he said, 'What is it, Peter?'

Peter laughed – a booming, brutal laugh that hurt Jesus' ears and roused his anger once more, 'I thought,' said Peter, 'that perhaps you had dropped off to sleep.'

'No,' said Jesus. 'I'm awake.'

When he finally did look up, he saw that Peter's big, round head had interposed itself, like some maleficent planet, between his eyes and the familiar heavens. Peter was a big-boned man. His thick-skulled head was covered with hair like coarse grass, and his rotund face ran to fat in the jowls and neck. His chin was blue-black with the new growth of ferocious stubble on it. Peter's eyes were very dark and deep-set and they glittered with drunken stupor.

'What is it that you wanted, Peter?'

Peter laughed again, even more loudly than before. His fingers squeezed Jesus' shoulder tightly. 'What a miserable specimen you are, after all,' he said, his voice thickening with phlegm. 'I don't understand it, I really don't. You were another man entirely when we were out in the desert and in the caves. You were passionate; you were articulate; you had ideas, plans. You were a real leader in every sense of the word. But in the past few weeks, since we've come into the towns, since we made up our minds to come right into Jerusalem and get something going, you've changed. You're all but unrecognizable, man. I don't understand what's come over you, or got into you, or transformed you. You're not even a caricature of a leader any more. Frankly, I don't know why we ever chose you.'

'You never chose me,' said Jesus as he twisted out of the other's grip. 'I was the one who made the choice.'

Peter swayed on his feet and held to the table to keep his balance. 'You must be joking, no? Your choice, indeed! Now I've heard everything! But, listen, what's the difference? Why should we quarrel during the holiday? I hire a house and pay for a Passover service and we begin an argument. It's too ridiculous!'

Peter leaned closer once more and Jesus was engulfed in the rank smell of his breath, which wheezed out in short spurts, as if some force were squeezing it out of Peter in spite of himself. His body exuded a sourness that seemed to Jesus the sourness of the world.

'Listen, old man,' Peter wheezed, 'we need to dress the evening up with a word from you. Something. Anything. You can't expect to sit here all night long at a Passover celebration and get by on your good looks. Be reasonable. Try to be your old self. Get some of that fire back. Give us some sort of speech!'

'What do you want me to say?'

Peter's whole body shook in a laugh that ended in a thin, jackal-like whine. 'Freedom,' he sneered. 'Why don't you talk about freedom?'

FIVE

The servant girl knew she was asleep, knew she was dreaming, and wanted to escape but could not. She struggled to awaken, prayed that she would come awake, but could not. She was doomed to the dream. In it, she wandered at night in the Valley of Kidron, outside the walls of the city, where she had as much to fear from Roman patrols as from roaming bands of outlaws. She tried to hurry on her way but some power drugged her limbs. Sweat stippled her face and dripped down her arms and back and ran between her breasts as if she were at work in the kitchen of her employer.

Suddenly, to her horror, she found that she was headed in a direction opposite the one that led home. She looked wildly about: if only she could find refuge from the nameless dread that pursued her. She tried to think, strained her mind as if against an icy, numbing current, but failed. She was lost, beset by forces which could not be perceived with her senses nor defined with her intelligence. She had lived a hard life, had endured much suffering, and was not given to moods of self-pity. She did not easily or frequently surrender to despair. But now, alone in the darkness of the valley, with a formless oppression crushing every resistance of mind and body, she grew dizzy and then sank to her knees.

The dust of the stony earth rose to her nostrils. She trembled for her life, fearing the sting of the scorpion and the strike of the asp; yet in truth she feared the power that sent the scorpion and the asp and the power that lurked in the darkness. It seemed she hovered at the edge of consciousness on the very brink of death.

And then something touched her shoulder. A shadow, from the vale of shadows? The light of a star, reaching down to her through luminous clouds? A wing? A paw? A human hand?

It was a voice that touched her. His voice.

She moaned in her sleep.

SIX

Jesus spoke to the assembly, saying, 'I've been asked by Peter to address you, though I should have preferred to keep silent. There are times when the heart is heavy beyond words and the tongue cannot carry what it has to say. I'm afraid tonight is such a time for me. . . .'

He paused, catching out of the corner of an eye the dark, impatient scowl of Peter. Then he looked down the long tables at the men who presumed to call themselves his disciples. At the far end, a couple of them were altogether stupefied with food and drink. Their heads were buried in the crooks of their arms or amongst the dishes. Jesus saw them suddenly as men without pasts, as men who blew about like tumbleweeds. He cleared his throat, and when he spoke once more his words were even fainter than before.

'We speak of freedom, my friends,' he said, 'but I wonder just how many of us dare to come truly face to face with freedom? Are we not, most of us, most of the days of our lives, frightened of freedom, terrified of its implications? To be free to accept or reject, embrace or rebel against, love or despise, implement or abstain from – are not these choices chilling to the very marrow of our bones?'

On his left, Andrew, a fat, ungainly man who had, it seemed to Jesus, increased his obesity and his ungainliness day by day since first the two of them had met, began to snore though sitting upright. His eyes were not properly shut even, but their surfaces were covered with a thick film that looked like ice formed from unclean water. Jesus stared at him, unable to resist the fascination. Andrew appeared to be both living and dead, and one wondered if vultures would not suddenly settle on his waxy flesh.

Jesus finally turned his gaze away. Of what use was life, earthly or other? Indeed, what life other than on earth could there be? Only a deluded or deranged mind could project the image of this world beyond the grave. Jesus stood silently at the head of the table. Breathing with difficulty, he observed the tangle of dishes, utensils, and leftover food on the table's filthy, spattered surface. Shielding his eyes from the sight, he leaned forward heavily on leaden legs.

'Go on,' said Peter. 'Go on and say something more. You haven't said a single thing worth hearing. Tell them about miracles. That's what they like to hear. And can you blame them?'

Jesus said, 'We seek our salvation in habit. We are afraid to accept the freedom of selfhood. We are fearful of the risk of free selves. We have blinded ourselves to nature, to its seasons, to its sap of life. We close our eyes to the leaves of death which blow against us. . . .'

Peter suddenly caught his arm. 'Wait,' he growled. 'Hold your tongue. I heard something.'

An owl screeched. Beneath the fig tree, the hound rose and trotted swiftly in the direction of the gate. Jesus heard the faint rattle of metal. From somewhere in the distance beyond the east wall of the courtyard, there came the tramping of feet in unison. The master of the house appeared in the doorway to the kitchen. The fire in the hearth behind him framed his large form in red.

Peter put his big hands on the table. 'Nobody open your trap,' he growled at the assembly, 'or I'll shut it for you. As sure as God made this earth, I will.'

Jesus did not say another word.

SEVEN

The young officer in command of the detachment dug his spurs into the flanks of his mount and rode several hundred yards in advance of the column of marching men. The light of the stars lay liquescent over the body of the cantering horse as it slipped forward through the night. Once, a hind hoof glanced off the dry skull of a wolf that lay in the dust of the road. The officer did not hear the hollow sound of the hoof striking the skull. He was far too absorbed in his thoughts.

He reined in the stallion on a knoll, where three or four stunted carob trees grew. Glancing quickly about him, he noted the surroundings. Ahead, the road to Gethsemane hugged the gentle curve of the hill. To the right, beyond the carobs, the knoll ended precipitously. The Valley of Kidron lay below. On the left there was a single, isolated house, with a fig tree that towered over its courtyard walls.

The officer turned the stallion and stared first at the house itself and then at the yard. No one appeared to be around. Except for the regular barking of a dog, he heard no other sound. It was all right, he thought.

The officer dismounted. Holding the reins casually, he gazed in the direction of Gethsemane. The horse bent its beautifully groomed neck to the earth, stretched out its head, and scattered with its breath the nearly rotten flakes of straw and dung.

The officer had broad shoulders and muscular, well-shaped arms and legs. His face was square-jawed with prominent bones, even features, and blue, unblinking eyes set shallowly under pale brows. His eyes never gave him away, he had a face that would not express anything openly. Only the heavy crude jaw gave hint of the grim stubbornness that stamped the man's life.

When the officer turned his head, pain shot through the back of his thick, close-shaven neck. The heat of Judean days, even in April, and the general filth of life in the country had produced a carbuncle there; the pain stabbed upward into the base of his skull and ran down into his shoulder blades. At times, it seemed to mingle with the pain in his mind.

As his men approached, his face betrayed no emotion whatsoever. Without warning, he jerked the stallion's head into the air; it whinnied with the cut and the insult of the bit. The approaching column flailed the road with the practiced beat of its feet and raised ghostly dust. Impatiently, the officer took a few steps forward to meet it and then stopped and raised his free hand. At the head of the formation, his second-in-command shouted an order over his shoulder and the rhythm broke off in the manner of a sharp cymbal clash. The subordinate stepped out and saluted; his superior seemed not to notice.

'You can proceed with the detail along the usual route,' the young officer said in a voice flattened by the constant issuance of commands. 'I'll catch up with you in due course.'

'Yes, sir.'

'And have Jannaeus fall out of ranks and stay behind. I wish a word with him.'

'Very good, sir.'

The second-in-command was an older man with grey streaked through his short beard. He turned and ordered Jannaeus out of the column. Then, marching backward, he again set the detachment in motion. The young officer stood rigidly off to one side and watched the column tramp off like a huge, ungainly caterpillar. Its joints clanked as it moved. When they were some distance away, the man began to sing in cadence; their meshed voices struck brutally at the silence of the night. Their song broke off as inexplicably as it had started; then they were out of sight, cancelled by the brow of the hill.

Jannaeus, scarcely breathing, stood stiffly at attention and stared directly to the front. The young officer was in no hurry to reach him. He walked slowly and calmly over to the man. The stallion followed closely behind. Without warning, he cocked back his arm and in a blindingly swift stroke struck Jannaeus full across his face with the slack length of the reins.

EIGHT

'Don't be afraid,' said Jesus, 'I'm with you.'

She lifted her head; it was lifted by a voice, soft and sad and full of longing. It floated down the mountain, sliding through the Garden of Gethsemane. It seemed to her like a spirit that was trying to materialize.

'Don't be frightened,' Jesus repeated. 'I'm here. Close by. I'll be down in a few moments.'

'No, no,' she gasped. 'That's all right. I'll come up to you. . . .'

She tried to catch sight of him in the swirling darkness but could not. She struggled to her feet and began to climb up the side of the mountain through the silvery, almost luminous, trunks of the olive trees. The ascent was steep and she kept slipping back and grasping at bushes and branches. A cold sweat broke out over her flesh. Her limbs grew heavy.

'I'm trying,' she called out. 'I'm coming. Don't leave me. I'll make it. . . .'

'I'm coming down to you,' he answered, but his voice sounded no closer.

'Please don't go away without me. Wait for me. . . .

'I'm here,' he called. 'Over here.'

But she could not see him. Ahead, just beyond her reach, was the low-lying branch of an enormous tree whose trunk loomed up from the earth like a fortress; she stretched out for it so that she could draw herself upward. She felt that she might then be able to see him moving down toward her. Her heart ached with dread and excitement. She lunged with her remaining strength.

But beneath her bare feet, a great section of earth broke away as if someone had bitten into it. She felt herself falling. Above her, the sky whirled like a smashed plate; the olive trees around her seemed to burn in silver flame; below her, a chasm yawned. She heard his voice calling again, but she could no longer make out what it said. She opened her mouth to scream.

21

NINE

Jesus heard the scream.

He wrenched himself out of Peter's grip and hurried across the courtyard. On orders of the master of the house, a servant had leashed the hound. Now as Jesus rushed past it, it writhed on its rope, howling and scattering gobs of spittle to the earth.

Jesus halted at the gate. He could see clearly across the knoll. There were two human figures on it and a horse. They were about two hundred yards away, and they were well defined in the moonlight. One of them knelt on the ground, as if at prayer, with his face buried in his hands; the other, holding the reins of the horse, stood over him. They were both Roman soldiers.

He could not hear what they were saying, but he sensed immediately the violence that had brought them to their postures. He knew how the scene would end unless somebody or something interfered. He wanted to walk out on the knoll, to raise a cry, to stop the thing before it took place. But he did not move. A torpor, a blind paralysis, came over him. He stood dizzily at the gatepost.

He felt impotent, cowardly, unreal. He wanted what he saw to be unreal. He wanted to destroy the reality he saw, to be safe, to be healed, to suck a woman's breasts, to be in the womb.

He wanted everything.

He did nothing.

TEN

The young officer's face was metallic, the colour of his helmet. His eyes brimmed with blackness as if the night had fled before the onslaught of the moon and sought refuge in them. He stood immobily and stared in silence as the soldier Jannaeus, humiliated because he had cried out when the reins had slashed across his face, lowered his hands. They were covered with blood that oozed from between his fingers and ran in thin rivulets down his bare forearms. Blood spurted from his nostrils; tears streamed from his eyes; his broken lips, swelling enormously, prevented him from uttering a word. As the shock of the blow grew less, he realized that he was on his knees, in the position of a supplicant, and he was ashamed.

The other took his eyes from Jannaeus for a moment and glanced down at the reins in his hand. They were metal-studded, and the studs were finely worked and polished. He was a little concerned that they might be damaged so he turned them over gently in his fingers and examined them. As he did so, some of the tremendous pressure that was building up within was siphoned off. Then he twitched the reins aside and turned his full attention to the soldier, who was trying to stop his nose from bleeding.

'Never mind that now,' said the officer. 'You'll have plenty of time for that sort of thing later on, if you're lucky.'

Jannaeus got unsteadily to his feet.

'That wasn't necessary either, soldier. Nobody instructed you to get up.' The officer flicked the loop of the reins at Jannaeus' chest: 'And keep your distance, pig! You stink of the dung heap!'

As if on its own accord, Janneaus' body started back. Again, he was ashamed.

Except for the unconscious twitching of a nerve in his left cheek, the young officer's face showed no emotion. He stood with his legs planted firmly apart and seemed to be lost in

23

private thought, as aloof to the man who faced him as he would have been to an insect. Actually, he was struggling to control an unbearable feeling of violence that welled up inside him like lava. It caused him pain that he could no longer separate from the intense throbbing of the boil on the back of his neck.

After a time, he said, 'Do you know why I have summoned you to this audience?'

The soldier Jannaeus tried to speak, but could not. He shook his head helplessly.

'Is this the manner in which you have been taught to respond to the question of an office in the army of Rome?'

He made as if to use the reins as a whip once more. The stallion backed off a step or two, preventing it, and the officer cursed it coldly without turning his head.

'Stay where you are, swine,' he said to Jannaeus, and then led the horse to a carob tree, where he fastened the reins to a lower branch. He returned slowly to his former position.

Jannaeus got a chance to collect himself. While the officer was busy with the stallion, he managed to staunch the blood at his nose and to dry his hands with some quickly scooped-up earth. He, like his commander, was a young man. He was slightly shorter than his superior, but also muscular and sturdy-limbed. His skull recently had been completely shaven – he found a bare scalp more comfortable in the fierce heat of the Judean hills – and the first needle-like hairs had begun sprouting once again over it: they itched, irritated by the sweat that stood forth over his head. He dared not remove his helmet to scratch.

His face was rounder than that of the officer. It had a cast of good humour and optimism about the mouth, a look that was also in his mild brown eyes. Now his face was swollen almost beyond recognition. His nose was turning black; Jannaeus sensed from the pain that it was surely broken. To his sorrow he thought that his face would be disfigured.

The soldier Jannaeus had been stationed in Judea for six months. He had been very homesick at first, but it had gradually passed away. He loathed the starkness of the Ludean land-scape, but he did not at all mind the Jews, whose constant fits of nervous energy and inscrutable religious ceremonies he puzzled

24

over without end. Sometimes he felt sorry for the Jews, though he was careful to keep the feeling to himself. Nor did he go around proclaiming the fact that he had no great love for soldiering. He was a conscript and he made the best of it, snatching whatever crumbs of pleasure and comfort he could take from the life.

As the officer came toward him, Jannaeus stiffened and tried to clear his mind; he knew that he would need all of his strength to deal with whatever ordeal was to come. On the officer's ornately engraved helmet and on the ornamentation of his scabbard, the moonlight flowed with sickly pallor. His footsteps sounded heavily on the earth of the knoll and even more heavily on the soldier Jannaeus' heart.

ELEVEN

She heard his footsteps in her dream.

They sailed into it like the arrows of the Roman archer units. Even before she had fully wakened and before her eyes could construe the true shape of the world, she had a sense of what they meant. Something warned her. She fumbled only momentarily in the straw – a chill of fear that she would not find it, that someone had stolen it while she slept, rising up her spine – and then, to her relief, her fingers closed around the bone handle of her knife. She turned on her pallet and held her breath. A shadow, groaning as it came, loomed over her; the breath hissed out of her lungs as she thrust the blade up at it.

The shadow leaped aside, cursing and spitting. She was able to make out its eyes now: they were pale husks of malice embedded like human fingernails in the darkness. She sat upright on her pallet, listening to the gasps of mingled rage and lust that came out of its invisible mouth and keeping the knife pointed at it.

'You could have killed me,' sobbed her half-brother. 'You could have killed me, you dirty bitch!'

'It's a damn shame I didn't, Simeon. The world would have been the better off for it.'

Now she could make him out more clearly. He was crouching just beyond the reach of her arm. Simeon was a thin, nervous, little watery-eyed man with crooked limbs and a face badly scarred by pox. A taciturn, moody, spiteful man, her half-brother was often away from home for weeks at a time; he spent much of his time hanging about the taverns and military posts, lending money, pimping, and doing odd jobs for Jews and Romans alike. There was nothing between the two of them except accident of family. Actually, the girl preferred the company of the listless, dying dog to that of the man.

'You think you're very clever, don't you?' he panted. 'Clever with the words you speak and clever with the knife you wield.

26

But you'll slip one of these days, yes, you'll make one little slip and then we'll see just how clever you really are. . . .'

'Stay away from me,' the girl whispered. 'You stink of wine and filth. Why don't you get back to your whores where you belong? If you dare to come near me again, I'll cut your throat from ear to ear, so help me God I will!'

The tone of her voice convinced him. Or perhaps it was the blade that danced out in front of her as she spoke, or perhaps he was overcome at last by the great quantity of wine he had consumed. She heard him slithering back across the earthen floor to his pallet, cursing foully as he went. Then her whole body began to shake, and she could not control it. She wanted to cry or faint, but did not permit herself the luxury of either.

TWELVE

It seemed to Jesus that someone had put a hole in his mind and that everything was rushing out through it. And it seemed to him, too, that something had happened to his body. The very life force in it was turning cold. He felt that he would soon become inanimate; that only the faintest point of awareness would be left hanging like a distant star above his corpse.

He was at the gate of the courtyard, but he did not feel he was himself. Selfhood seemed suddenly to be a meaningless idea. It was as if he were dissolved, as if memory, continuity, all that gave him an identity, were fading. He felt that he had dwindled and that the inscrutable forces about him had grown enormous.

When the officer left the kneeling figure of Jannaeus to tether the stallion, Jesus broke the invisible bonds that held him to the scene on the knoll and turned his head to look into the yard. The disciples were still at the table, although it seemed to Jesus that a thousand years had gone by. Several were asleep. One – he could not make out exactly who it was, but it looked like Andrew or Judas – slipped from his place before Jesus' eyes and fell heavily to the ground. Perhaps he had died? Perhaps the whole world was filled with corpses, who mistakenly thought themselves alive? Perhaps life was merely an illusion of the dead?

The yard seemed a landscape in a dream. Near the table a bucket lay on its side in the dust. In a far corner, a dark heap huddled on a pile of straw. He was the household idiot, who tended the cattle and earlier in the evening had shuffled about the Passover table until one of the servants had driven him off. The wall opposite was flooded with moonlight and looked as if it might melt at any moment. Jesus felt that he was a spirit and not a man.

Suddenly, the master of the house lurched into view. He was very tipsy, and he did a little dance as he moved his heavy body along, humming to himself and lifting his arms clumsily. Jesus saw him stoop to pick up a hefty stick from the earth. He rose slowly and continued to stagger across the yard. The whining hound came on its rope leash to meet him. But the animal's master, rising on his toes with surprising agility for so heavy and so drunk a man, struck it full in the face with his club. The dog seemed catapulted back. Its legs doubled up. It crouched in a womb of air. Then it lay sprawled at the base of the fig tree. The master of the house laughed and threw the club away.

Like a dreamer, Jesus stretched forth his hand. Nothing happened. Nothing changed. No one, himself included, was saved. His arm lay like a piece of driftwood in the air – the air through which the hound had sailed, the air under which his disciples sat and slept, the air beneath which the idiot lay, the air in which all who breathed would one day drown.

Jesus turned again to the knoll as he was seized. He recognized Peter and Thomas. Their winey breath blew in his face. Filled with revulsion, he called out for them to desist, but they pulled him from the gateway in behind the wall. Jesus struggled with them, and all three men fell to the earth.

'You crazy fool,' Peter said thickly. 'Do you want somebody to see you at the gate? That's all we need! Wasn't it enough that there were soldiers here? Are you looking for trouble?'

'Let me up,' Jesus said, choking in the dust.

For answer, Peter brought his beefy knee down on Jesus' neck.

THIRTEEN

The young officer's fingers were moving involuntarily toward the boil on his neck when he became aware of the fact and changed their direction completely. He frowned and touched his chin instead; then his hand dropped like a plumbline to the hilt of his sword where it rested comfortably, as if the power of the weapon flowed upward and lent it ease. His eyes looked Jannaeus up and down with their fixed, opaque stare.

'Now,' he said, 'we'll get somewhere at last. Tell me the truth: do you have any idea why I have detained you here tonight?'

The soldier Jannaeus struggled to work his swollen tongue; his lips opened and a fragment of broken tooth fell out.

'No, sir,' he said hoarsely.

'Well, then, I'll tell you in exactly two words, dog,' snapped the officer. 'The girl.'

Jannaeus was silent.

'Well, what have you to say to that? Do you have an answer? What is it? I'm waiting for your explanation. And by now you should know that it does not pay to make me wait.'

Still Jannaeus did not speak. A fresh surge of warm blood from a wound inside his cheek filled his mouth. He did not dare to spit; he had to swallow it.

'Is it that your tongue is no longer of any use to you? In that case, perhaps it would be better to remove it?'

The officer's hand and sword knew each other well. They were in perfect accord and did not have to think twice about their movements. The soldier Jannaeus saw a section of the blade appear, innocently white in the moonlight. The hiss of the sword's metal against the metal rim of the scabbard chilled his heart. He knew that he had to speak.

'Which girl do you mean?' he said. 'I do not understand, sir.'

'Surely,' said the officer, 'surely so young a man cannot have so old and deficient a memory? Come, come – you know the girl of whom I speak very well indeed. I first mentioned her to you more than a month ago – in the barracks yard. I warned you distinctly at that time to break off relations with her and to stay away from her altogether.' The sword slammed into the scabbard with a sharp crack that rolled across the silent knoll. 'But, I am sorry to say, the warning of an officer of the army of Rome meant nothing to you, absolutely nothing. I have been informed by reliable sources that you have been chasing after her again.'

Now it was clear to Jannaeus. The girl. Of course. The officer was enamoured of her. What he said was true. He had spoken to Jannaeus about her some time ago, but the soldier had forgotten the incident. He loved the girl; he had dismissed the officer's warning and pursued her, though she had not returned his attentions.

'Well,' said the officer, 'you are trying my patience sorely.'

The soldier Jannaeus had nothing to say. There was nothing to say. The meaning of this meeting on the knoll was coming home to him with slow, final clarity. Everything he saw – the moon, round and white as a wafer in the great space of the night sky; the centre carob and the stallion knocking fitfully against its trunk; a lone house over on the left, the gateway to its walled courtyard empty; the officer – himself like a sword drawn from the sheath – spoke to him with solemnity, with sadness, with the painful stamp of last farewell. It was as if at the very instant of departure he received the first understanding of what the world was about, what it truly meant. And now that he was beginning to understand, he did not want to leave. There had to be a mistake.

The soldier Jannaeus looked into the officer's eyes and knew there was no mistake. A light had flicked on the flint of their pupils: the lonely light of death. Jannaeus was too afraid to let himself know that he was afraid. He was young. He had no real experience with death. An uncle had died when he was a child. Neighbours in his city had been carried off by the plague. He had once seen a pedestrian crushed by the wheels of a wagon. Natural deaths, like the fall of leaves. He had never killed in

31

war; his unit had never been in combat. He was young and good-natured: killing was an abstract science in which he had little interest. He never wanted to kill, nor had anyone ever desired or attempted to kill him. Until now.

FOURTEEN

Until now.

She had waited until now, until this night, and she would wait no longer. She had herself under control. She had made her decision. Even if her half-brother was not asleep and came after her again, she would go. He would regret another attack. She would not hesitate to cut him, even to kill him.

She lifted herself from the straw and looked about the room. There was no movement; the other pallet was still. From the old man's place, she could just catch the faint whispering of his breath. Like the stiff-jointed dog, he seemed to be conversing with another world. She shivered and moved slowly onto the damp earth of the floor.

Bending low, she crept forward. Simeon moaned: she was certain that he took his malice with him into his dreams. At the door, she halted, much as she had before entering the hut. She realized she was leaving this place forever.

Her good memories were as few and as meagre as the bits of food littered about her father and the animal. She could take real pleasure only in knowing that though her life had been hard and bitter, it had not overcome her. She was still alive in the deepest senses of the word. Her hand reached out for the latch. She heard the half-brother stir and she froze and held her breath; the knife was ready in her hand. Silence again. Outside, she heard the caterwaul of a tomcat. The old man yawned in his sleep. He was probably dreaming of the food he had eaten this night and a meal like it that he would have in the future.

Then she thought of her mother, whom she had not thought of in years and whom she had scarcely known. As a very young woman, the mother had lost her first husband; he had been slain in the gutter like a stray dog by a Roman cavalry officer who claimed that the Jew had insulted and attacked him. She soon after married the girl's father, an older man. She had died when the girl was still a child, wasting away day by day like a wax figure. The girl did not weep; she only remembered with sadness. Even then the sorrow seemed to be distant, to have little to do with her.

She determined to leave this place and to seek out the man at the Passover table of whom she had dreamed. He spoke no more than a few words to her during the entire evening; he, indeed, scarcely noticed her. But there was something in a look he gave her, something which aroused longing and promise. She would find him and ask to go with him, wherever he went. If he refused, if he proved to be merely another phantom, she would take to the road. Nowhere it led could be as insufferable as was this place. And if all else failed, if there were no place for her on this earth, there was always the door of death waiting for her to open.

She pulled the latch.

FIFTEEN

The disciple who had fallen to the ground from his place at the table was not at all a cadaver. He was yet Judas, the living man, and as he lay on the earth of the courtyard his thoughts carried him back to the days of his childhood; and his heart laughed and overflowed with joy.

He lay with a smooth cheek in the same dust into which Jesus had been shoved, and he lay with a broad smile on his lips. He had passed out in alcoholic stupor; the fumes of the numberless glasses of strong wine he had drunk had snuffed out his consciousness. But layers beneath his stupor there was a tunnel that kept twisting back to his childhood, and it was down that winding tunnel he had disappeared.

In Judas' dream, the sun shone brightly in a sky of kiln-glazed blue. It was the time of the spring planting and the fields were fragrant; over the earth the oxen slowly moved, the plows they pulled opening the dark pod of the soil in long, straight furrows. Far in the distance, across the valley, flocks of sheep grazed on the grassy flanks of the hills; when the shepherds moved them, they bunched together, flowerlike, and when they wandered apart to crop, they were like scattered petals.

Judas ran down to the brook with two other children, a boy and a girl of his own age. The wind stirred their hair and tickled their faces as they ran. In the hollow, where the water splashed over glistening rocks, it was cool and secret; they liked to sit there and watch for hours. They looked into a pool where the light pointed melting fingers into its mysterious depths. Sometimes, the silver-dark shadow of a fish flashed by. On the bank, the grass was tall and sweet; over it, orange and black butterflies skimmed. The green branches of a tall willow streamed down like tears of joy; sparrows flitted to and from them. In a meadow nearby, cows lowed.

There were three reflections in the pool whenever they bent

over it to drink. Judas' was in the centre. His hair was fair; his eyes were blue; his smile was brilliant. His chin was dimpled. Over his shoulder, the sun blazed like a stack of new-mown hay in the sky; it crowned his head with a halo of gold and he could not take his eyes away from that dazzling image in the water. His heart brimmed with gladness and he laughed out loud.

SIXTEEN

Scenes of his childhood streaked through Jannaeus' mind like
falling stars. They were random scenes over which he seemed
to have no control. His young mother and his sister sat before
the hearth, mending clothes, on an autumn afternoon. A quiet,
sunny street at noon in the summertime, with the village dogs
curled up asleep in the skimpy shade of blue-green cypresses. A
dusty, bumpy ride in a hay-filled cart to another town down the
river with the smell of the hay making him dizzy and the sky
overhead looking like an enormous pond in which white clouds
swam. His father lifting him high up in his arms, high among
the leaves of a birch that glittered in late afternoon sun like
coins; his father sitting by the wayside and drinking wine from
a goatskin.

The soldier Jannaeus forgot death altogether. But it did not
forget him. It lunged out of the young officer's eyes and compelled him to pay attention to it once more.

The officer, Jannaeus thought, was really wrong. He had not
actually disobeyed the officer's warning and command; he had
simply, in the course of things, forgotten that such a command
existed. He had stayed away from the girl for a short time, but
he had been unable to resist her. The girl was a star he was
compelled to follow. He had not dreamed she would be his
death star.

He knew this was death even when his mind betrayed him. It
told him no and kept summoning up scenes of long ago, scenes
that could never be recaptured or relived, scenes that were inconsequential odds and ends. They smiled at him from the
infinite depths of memory. They tried to make him believe that
he was safe among them, that they would protect him. He heard
the favourite song his mother sang while she prepared food for
the family. A flight of starlings wheeled in a wintry sky. A
friend's dog sniffed a crust in the dust of the road. A group of
harvesters, covered with straw, trooped home from the fields,

the curved blades of their scythes orange in the last rays of the sun. The waves of memory cast up these pictures, wanting to assure him that both the scenes and he were eternal. They told him of no blood, no pain, no sorrow, no grave. He knew they lied.

Jannaeus saw the officer's cheek twitch convulsively. It looked to him as if a wound were suddenly opened there and just as suddenly closed. He saw that the officer's whole body had gone taut, as if a dark force were screwing the flesh ever more tightly on its frame of bones.

Jannaeus watched as the officer, breathing deeply, drew his sword.

SEVENTEEN

Jesus' eyes closed. He was glad to shut out the world. The bodies of Peter and his cohort pressed down on him. This was fitting because his whole life weighed heavily on him. The disciples and their hysteria; the meetings and their inevitable confusion; the endless, empty speeches; the meaningless plans; the incidents full of frustration and contradiction: they galled him. They all fit together in the mosaic of his mind to form a nightmarish picture. Things had begun well; they were falling apart now; they would end badly. The men whom he most trusted could no longer trust themselves. They were bewildered, fearful, and bitter. They grasped at any evil straw that blew their way. They turned into charlatans and fanatics and wanted him for their fetish. They would not get him.

He shut his eyes even more tightly, and the world of the disciples vanished at his will. He saw before him once more the face of his mother, mysterious as the full moon. Her sad eyes told him nothing; they asked for help. But there was nothing he could do for her or anyone. Even the person, or entity, he claimed to be was in reality a battleground for many opposing forces, and he could not forecast the struggle's end. His mother's lips curled. A bitter, accusing look came over her features. She seemed to stare at him reprovingly. But why? He was not the cause of her bitterness; he did not put the look of unhappiness in her eyes. What then did she want of him? What did she think he could give her? He was baffled, and so he had left her hearth.

His father was only a shadow. The more he stretched forth his arms to the man, the more elusive the man became. It was true that he was stitched through Jesus' infancy and early childhood, but the thread was a delicate one and it broke off every time Jesus lifted the fabric to examine it. The man had given Jesus the gift of life but he had not stayed to explain just why he had conferred it. Once again, Jesus was puzzled. It did not seem to him that the puzzle had a solution. Or even a name.

Jesus sighed with weariness. He had covered this sterile ground so many times before. He wished desperately to sleep, but could not. Instead, he saw himself as once more a very young man in Galilee. In his fantasy, he stood at the top of a hill and yet stood in the valley at its foot. It was the time of early spring. Almond blossoms were scattered on the rain-softened earth. The thickets pulsed with green buds. From the uppermost branches of a copse of eucalyptus trees, crows flew screaming. Pale irises thrust up from the ground. Lazy clouds drifted in the sky.

Jesus stood on the height and in the low place at the same time. How could it be? He did not understand. He did not want to accept it, but he had no power to change it. His heart ached that he might join himself together, but he remained divided.

Along the road that ran between the two places where he stood, a Roman cohort moved. At its head, a force of cavalry rode; and one brought up the rear. Between the horsemen marched a column of infantrymen; they wore heavy mail and bore large shields and spears whose points ran together to form a long, undulating bed of nails in the air. Out in front, at a distance from the main body of soldiers, rode the commanding officers and their standard-bearers. On the embossed helmets of the commanders, the plumes tossed jauntily; the standards glittered in obsequious sunlight. The hum of marching soldiers floated across the fields.

Jesus watched in silence. Among the olive trees on the hillside, workers lifted their heads; farmers looked up from their furrows; the crows flew shrieking into the sky and were promptly swallowed by its mouth.

Jesus started. At the roadside were his mother and father. His mother wore a black shawl, whitened by the dust of a long journey. Jesus saw the tears glistening like the spearheads of the soldiers on her cheeks, but could do nothing. His father smiled enigmatically up at him and was instantly struck from his place by the butt of a warrior's spear as the column went by; he tumbled backward, still smiling, into the weeds and lay so on his back. Blood gushed from his mouth. Flies large as raisins settled over the parted lips and protruding tongue.

Directly in the column's path, an infant played happily. The knot of officers and standard bearers on their magnificent steeds trampled it to pulp. The line of cavalry and footmen made it one with the dirt. Where the baby had been, there was only a dark, wet spot. Not even the flies touched it. Jesus stood above and below, yearning to coalesce, waiting for a sign of life to appear where the infant had been murdered. He sought an iris or even a single blade of grass. He felt such a sign might give him unity.

The workers in the olive groves and the farmers in the fields took up their tools and went home. His mother and father disappeared. The sun sank and it got dark. Jesus waited and there was nothing. A single star rose in the heavens and he hoped it was the infant, but it was not. It was only a dead stone in the sky.

EIGHTEEN

The door of the hovel closed behind her. She was out in the narrow street. The moon was shining. She walked quickly away from the house and did not look back. She would be free or die in the attempt.

She chose a route back to her master's house where she hoped to find the man who had been at the Passover table. She was afraid, but the memory of that man's face helped her overcome her fear. Under its spell, she felt her mind grow sharp and steady; her heart grow more fierce and yet more calm. And she felt her body, which had always spoken to her with a special, secret import, fill with new life, almost with a will of its own.

Her back bore the faint scars of the old man's canes – faint because he had not had the strength to use them on her in many years. Her left wrist carried her half brother's tooth marks, souvenir of the quarrel he once had picked with her. Her right thigh was bruised black and blue from a blow dealt by the truncheon of a Roman soldier 'keeping order' in the marketplace a week ago. But her body was good and lithe and pure and now, on her way to him, it burned like an east wind from the desert.

At the first thoroughfare, the clatter of an approaching detachment of soldiers filtered down the street. She darted into the shadow of a housefront. She pressed against the stone façade: soldiers were always trouble; at night, they were deadly. The leader swung into view. Behind him was the bearer of the standard. In the light of the moon, they had the greenish pallor of dead men.

As they came closer, she started. She recognized the standard and then the man at the head of the column. He was an old man with greying hair and a paunch, a junior officer. He marched with a bearing born of long habit, but the swagger had gone from his gait and the ardour from his eyes. He would die for his emperor and for his superiors, but he would do it on command with a quiet cynicism that would never reveal itself openly.

She knew him and she knew his direct superior. The very thought of the latter made her hug the wall more closely. He was a young man who could not be said to have any age or sex. He was a creature so remote and detached that he seemed to have come to Judea not from somewhere in the Roman empire but from another world. Yet he had shown her that he wanted her. She resisted him as she had resisted the others: but she feared him as she feared none of the others. Now, as she clung to strange stones in the night, she dreaded seeing him as never before. He might as well have been the angel of death.

He was sometimes at the head of the column, and other times at its rear, prodding a straggler with the point of his sword, or using his horse – as she had seen him do many times – for the same purpose. He had spoken few words to her, but she understood what he wanted. He waited for her to give it to him; if she did not, he would move in and take it by force. She knew that he felt it was his earth, his sky, his empire, his world – and that he could take by force anything which did not yield to his will.

Pressing against the stones that still preserved some of the dampness of yesterday's rain, she breathed as shallowly as she could and watched the soldiers pass. The rear of the column was in sight. In spite of herself, she trembled and hated herself for it. She had resolved to use her dagger if she had to – on him or on herself.

But he was not at the column's rear. A lanky non-commissioned officer, looking half-asleep on his feet, was the last man of the detachment. Still, she did not move from her hiding place. She did not dare. She knew he was capable of every sort of trickery. Perhaps he had spotted her somehow and was merely waiting for her to show herself before sweeping down on her astride his infernal horse. Perhaps he was watching her at this very moment. He wanted her and for his own private reasons he played a game with her. She could not stop trembling.

It took a long time for her to calm down. At last she did and stepped out of the shadows. The moon still shone down. The sounds of the marching column had long faded from the tunnel of the street. She stared in the direction it went and then took the opposite one.

NINETEEN

'I have an excellent solution,' said the young officer. 'Yes, I really think I can solve your extremely serious problems. I do firmly believe that this sword in my hand will cure you of all of your maladies: at one and the same time, and for all time!'

The officer knew that all his life, the soldier Jannaeus had been taught obedience. He was aware that the training had begun in early childhood and continued pervasively, without a stop. But he knew that the sight of his naked sword had severed the bond to it in one stroke. Out of the corner of his eye, the officer saw Jannaeus' shield and spear: they had been flung to earth a half dozen yards away by the force of the blow he had dealt the soldier. He knew Jannaeus had no chance to retrieve them. He fathomed that the soldier's mind now worked feverishly, struggling against the wish to deny what faced him, against random thoughts that trembled like dry leaves, against indolence, against surrender, against paralyzing fear of the man opposite him. He knew Jannaeus would do anything in order to stall for time, in order to give his mind a chance to function, to puzzle things out, to devise any plan.

'I did not even begin to realize,' Jannaeus said, wincing with pain as he spoke, 'That the girl meant so very much to you, sir. Had I known, had I the faintest inkling this was, so, sir, I should have never set eyes on her again—'

And as Jannaeus spoke the words, the officer saw how the soldier's fingers slowly crept toward the dagger in its sheath on his belt. He had remembered, of course, during his terrible search for a way out, that the knife was there. He thought he would get it out stealthily: get it out and use it, swiftly and to the mark, as he had been taught by officers such as the one who faced him. The officer caught every movement of the fingers as Jannaeus' right hand slid up the sheath to the metal handle of the dagger.

'It was sheer folly which I engaged in, sir. I never should have dreamed of pursuing the girl had I a true idea of what she meant to you,' Jannaeus said, as he gradually drew the knife out. 'On my very life, and on my honour as a subject of Rome and a soldier of the army of Rome—' And then the dagger was out, free of its case, ready to strike. The officer almost smiled.

But then he scowled. The fool's fingers had betrayed him. Perhaps they had learned the lesson of blind obedience too well and could not forget it. They failed. And Jannaeus' knife lay foolishly in the dust at his feet. Perhaps, at the crucial moment, his mind wandered; perhaps he thought of the girl, whom he so foolishly loved; perhaps he wondered how the mystery of his birth had brought him to this forlorn knoll in Judea; perhaps his nerve went when he needed it most; perhaps he was incapable of killing the officer or anyone; perhaps his mind and his fingers did not like each other and did not care to work together; perhaps the fatal eyes of his enemy had struck him down; perhaps he felt it all wasn't worth it. The officer sneered inwardly. Jannaeus' dagger now lay in the dust. It had fallen without a sound. But the young officer, having seen all, also heard the sound it did not make.

The officer's eyes did not change. But he laughed and his strong, even teeth shone.

'Pick it up,' he said. 'I don't kill a man without a weapon in his hand. You do me a gross offense to imagine so. Pick it up, carrion. Though you don't deserve it, I'll give you a chance to defend yourself.'

Jannaeus blinked. His jaw shook. His knees were weak but he bent, without a word, to retrieve the dagger. The back of his young, strong neck gleamed whitely in the moonlight. The officer saw on it the exact spot where the carbuncle was on his own neck. In his mind, the pain leaped like a flame of white pus. He lifted himself on his toes. His right arm pumped up through the air, and he brought the sword whistling down with all his force into the soldier Jannaeus' bared flesh. It shattered the vertebrae and cut clean through the neck and out, almost striking to the earth below. A great fount of blood spurted forth. The head fell away, bounding softly in the dust and rolling over and over like a ball of bloody meat with hideously bulging eyes. It stopped face down and the officer was pleased that he had no longer to look at its ugliness.

He wiped his sword carefully on Jannaeus' tunic and returned it in that motion to its scabbard. Then he lifted the dripping torso and bore it, legs dangling, to the far end of the knoll. With a single, short grunt he cast it over the edge into the valley. Then he returned for the head and the helmet. He flung them both far out into the chasm. Then he brushed his hands, walked over to the carob tree, untethered the stallion, and mounted it with a curse. He struck its flank savagely with the loose end of the reins and galloped down the road.

The pain was gone from his mind.

TWENTY

Jesus opened his eyes. Had he heard something? Or was it merely an echo of the scream he heard before? Or was it his own mind that had screamed? He looked around. The court-yard was white and silent under the moon; it looked as if snow had fallen. From the oleander thickets by the house, cicadas sang. Beyond the wall, an owl hooted twice. To his right lay Peter and the other on the ground. One sprawled on his back, the other on his belly. They appeared bloodless in the moonlight like corpses abandoned on the field of battle.

Jesus got up carefully: he did not want to waken the dead. Nothing stirred. The servants had gone long ago. The disciples slumped over the table and benches. He remembered the knoll and went over to the gate. Nothing was to be seen. Whatever had happened could not be undone. Then he remembered the dog and walked over to the fig tree.

The animal's lifeless carcass seemed half the size of the living dog; it was beginning to grow stiff. The muzzle was mangled; the forehead had been completely crushed by the club. The dog's eyes were wide open and glassy, with two tiny points of light swimming uselessly in them. The mouth was open too. In the morning it would be stuffed with flies.

He stood and thought about the dog. It was dead, but it was also, at last, free of its master. Jesus was alive; he was not free. For the first time in many years, perhaps for the first time in his entire life, he had both a chance to be free and the desire to do so. He looked around the yard once again and smiled sadly. The men who at first needed and harboured him and then hedged and hemmed him in, the men who at first were his helpers and then his jailers, the men who initially tried to understand and later chose to misinterpret, the men who in the beginning had the courage to question and in the end took to fearing the answers now, this Passover night, fell prey to their own weaknesses.

And so the man, Jesus, who had fallen victim to them, was free.

TWENTY-ONE

Simeon slept badly. He dreamed that he entered a cave, lost his way, and could not get out. Strange, luminous insects hung in the darkness about him and crawled across his path. His ears caught the sound of distant, sorrowing voices. He was certain he would find an exit. But as time passed and he did not, he became discouraged and then frightened. A terrible thirst came over him. He heard water trickling everywhere about him, but could discover none.

Suddenly, down at the end of what appeared to be a long corridor of rock, he saw light. He moved toward it, stumbling, banging his head on projecting spits of rock, and tearing his fingers on sharp rock edges. As he went forward, he was able to discern a figure in the distant nimbus. He recognized his half-sister. She was clad as if the king himself had clothed her for some regal event. She laughed. She drank continuously from a goblet that did not have to be refilled.

Simeon's eyes narrowed. His parched lips sucked the cindery air. His fingers clawed the flanks of the tunnel for support. In the cage of ribs imprisoning it, his heart pounded. He was filled with ungovernable rage. He knew that when he reached the girl, he would throttle her with his bare hands. Yes, he would strangle her even before he satisfied his thirst, because his loathing for her was greater than it.

He quickened his pace. Nothing would stop him. No, he would not even touch the goblet from which her hated lips drank. He would choke the life from her, fling her body to the floor of the cave, smash the goblet, cut her throat with a shard of it, and empty her vessels of their blood by drinking it. He would watch her figure shrivel, and then he would fling aside the remains like a rag. He would press his mouth to the cleft in the rock wall from which all of the water in the world came and drink for as long a time as he chose.

But he seemed to get no nearer to her. And when he

screamed out at her and told her what he meant to do to her when he caught hold of her, she vanished in a flash of cold, unearthly fire. He stopped. All was utter blackness. He was frozen with terror. He cried out and the echoes of his voice whipped back at him, terrifying him more. He dropped to his knees. Nausea overwhelmed him; his body shook as with fever. Then, in the figures of the rock he knelt on, a glowing red wound appeared: a raw, scarlet slit which had no name and no mercy and would in the end swallow him alive.

He awoke from the dream in a cold sweat. He was awake in time to hear the door close as his half-sister left. He rose immediately to pursue her.

TWENTY-TWO

There was nothing to keep him any longer. Jesus turned from the body of the dog and began to walk slowly toward the gate when he heard a low moan. He turned.

Puzzled, Jesus again started for the gate. But the moans returned. They were low and strangely urgent. Surveying the yard carefully, Jesus realized at length that they came from the idiot asleep in a far corner. He went over.

Jesus had seen the idiot when the *Seder* began. He was a small, misshapen man, with vacant eyes, long dangling arms, and a shuffling gait. One of the servants said he was the illegitimate son of the master of the house and a fieldworker who had disappeared shortly after the birth; another claimed he was the offspring of a servant who had saved the master's life when he was a small child and had herself been struck down in the act. The men at the Passover table had given him scraps of food at the start of the meal, but the master had ordered him to be driven off to his corner.

Jesus looked down and saw that though the man did not appear to be fully awake, something had frightened him, perhaps a nightmare. He lay on his back in a pile of rags and straw, an arm flung across his face as if to ward off a blow. His hair was matted with filth. A long, lumpy scar crossed his forehead. Jesus bent down, and the man moaned once again and flung out the arm. His eyes rolled open, showing only their whites, and a violent shudder passed through his frame.

Jesus watched him shake and wondered what hand shook him as if he were already a skeleton. He bent closer and peered at the idiot's face. It was small, triangular, and slightly elongated, laced deeply with wrinkles and spotted with old and running sores. A hairy mole, like a black beetle, grew off the point of the chin. The large nostrils flared out, looking like raw wounds that had been punched into the visage by spikes. To

Jesus, it appeared to be the face of a foetus or a dead man or a mask worn for a pagan festival.

And then it became for Jesus a mirror in which he could see his own face. Without illusion, without recoil, without hope, he gazed into the face. As if he were calmly looking down from the stars above him, he saw the awful pain of all flesh and its bafflement, its dissolution, its total obliteration. He saw the earth itself as a great, fleshy face, all warted and lined and run with scabs: the face of an idiot.

Jesus reached down and touched the man's shoulder.

'Can you speak to me?' he said. 'Can your flesh talk?'

The idiot moaned softly. His rank breath touched against Jesus' face. He had soiled himself and a terrible stink arose from him. His bare feet twitched in the straw. His tongue swam muddily in his mouth. He seemed to gasp for breath and then recover.

Jesus withdrew his hand. He had no answer. He had only the blindness of this man's fate and the blindness of his own heart. He knew no excuse. He felt that only silence could scream out the unscreamable within him. Without awareness of it, he dug his fingers into the flesh of his palms.

And then Jesus saw the eyes of his mother and they seemed to be of stone. His father hovered over him like an evil ghost. And then he beheld a strange woman with breasts of flint. He drew near unto her and saw that she had in her body a terrible wound which oozed blood like slow, black tears. He fell upon his knees before her and wanted to cry out, but his eyes remained dry. And then the wound dilated and uttered words: 'No mercy,' it seemed to say.

And then the idiot whimpered again. Jesus saw that his face was covered with sweat, and he touched the face and felt that it was cold. The idiot's body shuddered convulsively. His breath came in short, hard gasps. Jesus quickly removed his cloak and wrapped the trembling body in it. Then he rose and left the courtyard.

TWENTY-THREE

She encountered only one other Roman patrol. It was a small, city patrol and she avoided it with ease because its members were preoccupied with a suspect they had picked up a short while before. They had surrounded the man and were working him over with the shafts of their spears and the flats of their swords. His screams rang through the stone corridor of the street, echoing on each other and building into an eerie fugue. Not a door or shutter opened. Only dogs, as frightened as their masters, answered his cries. The soldiers grunted at their work. She slipped by easily.

The gate of the courtyard was ajar. No servant came forward to meet her. The hound was silent. The fig tree, the walls of the yard, the side of the house were all bathed in moonlight. The dormant men at the Passover table looked like blocks of granite sunk into a spectral sea. She was uneasy. Was he still there?

She crossed the yard and peered at the men slumped over the table. He was not among them. Several were on the ground; she went over to them. The last was Peter who lay on his back in the grip of an erotic dream. His robe had become disarrayed and his half-tumescent member was exposed; it was large and bulbous like a rotten turnip. She looked away.

She went from him to the house's master who lay asleep by the evergreen. Several feet from him, she discovered the dead dog. It lay in deep shadow, out of the white moon glaze on the turf, as if the night wished to hide it from sight. She was alarmed and rushed to the kitchen.

The fire was low; only a single log pulsed with flames among grey ash. Some of the house servants, too weary and drunk to go to their pallets, had curled up on the hearth. She skirted them and searched through the house. He was nowhere to be found.

Out in the yard again, she heard the idiot moan and ran to him. She recognized the cloak instantly and dropped to her

54

knees, the blood hammering at her temples. Then she saw the idiot's masklike face. She shook her head uncomprehendingly. How did he come to be wearing the other's cloak? And where had the other man gone?

'Where is he?' she whispered. 'Tell me where he went.'

The idiot opened his eyes and saw her. A look of terror came over his countenance. His tongue thrashed out a stream of unintelligible sounds.

TWENTY-FOUR

Simeon pitched himself headlong into the bushes just in time; a second later, his half-sister came running through the gate. Crouching behind the budding branches, he watched her turn to the left and hurry down the road, its dust spurting in little, mercury-white puffs at her heels. He was not surprised. He thought her a madwoman and nothing that she did really surprised him. Her life was quite incomprehensible to him, but it did not matter. He did not have to understand what he wanted to destroy.

Soon she was swallowed by distance, though there was nowhere she could go to escape him. The road led down across the Valley of Kidron to Gethsemane, on to the Mount of Olives, and then back again to Kidron and into the city. He could easily intercept her by a shorter route if he wished to. But he did not want to kill her by dark: it would take her unaware, mean nothing to her, and thus little to him. He wanted her to taste his anger gradually, so that its full intensity would not be wasted. He wanted her to perish with a complete knowledge of his hatred.

He regarded the open gate out of which she had come. No one seemed to be guarding it. The courtyard and house were dark and silent. Something very strange was happening; he felt it in his bones. He rose and peered carefully about him. His ears were cocked for the sound of a patrol, a watchman, or a dog. He heard nothing that aroused suspicion. The moon stared down coldly at him. About it, the stars shot out tiny forked tongues of bluish light.

Cautiously, he made his way out of the brush and crossed the road to the gate, ready to kick any watchdog that rushed out to meet him. There was no challenge. The blood churned through his veins. His breath came quickly. Had he truly stumbled onto something? Would this night reward him beyond his dreams? Still, he did not go through the gate. He had been duped many times in his life and he did not want to take a chance. He did not relish the thought of being turned over to the authorities.

Finally, he decided to act. He moved quietly and swiftly into the yard. His wiry, little body was taut; his small, red-rimmed eyes darted about and took stock of everything. He knew an animal had been killed and he wasted no time thinking about it. His attention focused on the human figures. He sensed that they all slept the sleep of the stupefied and he breathed more easily. Beetlelike, he moved over the ground on his thin, bowed legs. At the table, he snatched up a carafe of wine recklessly and drank greedily; it dribbled down his chin and leaked onto his dusty tunic.

Smacking his lips, he set the vessel down. At the other end of the table, one of the disciples stirred. Simeon froze. The man soon lapsed once more into a deep slumber. The half-brother's breath hissed from him. He was reassured; all was well. The fumes of the strong wine mounted heavily to his brain. A wild desire to laugh out loud, to howl with disdain came over him, but he stifled it. Instead, he began moving with extraordinary rapidity from figure to figure, expertly going through their garments with spidery fingers. The disciples had a few coins among their number, but Peter carried a fat purse. He sighed as it was taken from him, just as if he were giving up the ghost, and Simeon grinned. His feet almost danced a jig on the earth. The wine fanned a fire in him: he felt bold and cheerful. He was certain this was a night he would long remember. He forgot his half-sister completely and staggered across the courtyard toward the master of the house.

TWENTY-FIVE

In Peter's dream, he drifted through water lilies slowly downstream on a raft. He lay supine, lulled by a deep sense of well-being. His body was white as the flat, thick petals of the lilies; as soft as butter, and smooth-textured as cream. From the cloudless sky above, a warm sun laved its nakedness and aroused it with a lascivious warmth. In slumber Peter smiled.

He had plump, pudgy fingers which went well with the plumpness of his figure. He lifted them before his face and gazed raptly at them, almost as if he were discovering them for the first time. The nails were pared carefully; the cuticules were fresh-looking and pink, and they shone in the bright sunlight like polished stones. Each finger looked like a male sex organ: the sudden thought increased his erotic pleasure.

Peter placed his fingers gently on his neck and then on his chest; drowsily, he caressed his nipples and then his hairless stomach. He adored his stomach which rose sweetly from his chest like a hill of satin. He was in ecstasy. His eyelids were heavy as rainbow prisms played over their lashes. His lips parted and from the carmine chalice of his mouth the breath delicately bubbled forth.

Below the hillock of his belly, his pubic hair was a fleecy arrowhead pointing downward. He ran his fingers lightly through it. He laughed breathlessly. Erect over the twin, wrinkled white frogs of his testicles was his member, the only discoloured part of his otherwise blemishless body. Its purple head was asymmetrical; its stem was angrily red and run lengthwise by shiny, twitching veins. Peter dared not touch it: it was far too holy. He could readily imagine it an object of worship.

He blinked. Was there a cloud in the sky? He looked puzzled. A spot stained the brilliant blue shield of the sky; it rushed toward him, growing larger as it came. After a time, he could see that it was the figure of a man and that the man was Jesus. Through the air Jesus flew, his hair streaming back, his cloak billowing out after him. One hand was upraised; in it, something glittered brightly. Peter thought that Jesus was carrying a sceptre and that he was approaching that he might anoint him, but then he saw that Jesus bore in his upraised hand a knife.

Peter was stricken with terror. The sense of the matter was clear. His naked erection was a beacon certain to attract the metal moth of a blade. His flesh crawled as he cringed and tried to roll from the raft. He found he could not move from his back: it was as if he had been nailed to it. His fingers leaped toward his organ that they might protect it but again he was foiled. It was sacred and his hands were paralyzed by its binding power.

'No,' Peter cried out. 'Oh no!'

But his voice was as the croaking of the frogs in the rushes of the banks and among the pad islands of the lilies. He looked about madly, unable to rise or in any manner defend his loins. His eyes bulged from their sockets. He saw that the lilies had all sprouted phalluses and that Jesus was walking swiftly across the water of the stream, stooping and slashing with his knife at the upright members. The razor-sharp blade flashed in the sun as the organ stalks scattered to the right and left, each severed at its thick base from the soft green pad below. With ejaculatory force blood shot up from each gaping wound, ran into the limpid water, and reddened it.

Jesus came toward Peter. He scowled as he bent and wielded the knife in a great, glittering arc.

TWENTY-SIX

The young officer recounted his story.

The post commander, a short, stocky man in his early fifties, sat and listened restlessly, though he did not show it. He had quarrelled violently that afternoon with his mistress, a red-haired Jewess with a temper like a bobcat and fingernails to support it, and had the taste of bile in his mouth ever since. Toward the end of the report, when he gathered its significance, he rose heavily from his seat and headed for the latrine, turning his head to growl back permission for the younger officer to take whatever action he deemed necessary.

The young officer wasted no time. He intimately knew the soldiers of the post. Striding into the barracks, he picked a dozen of the best cavalrymen, and roused them from sleep by brutally squeezing their arms. As he hurried off to the stable to get himself a fresh mount, the soldiers rose, cursing, and struggled into uniform. The officer waited for them on the parade ground, gazing impassively up at the stars, which looked like the heads of silver nails that had been driven into the vast dome of the sky.

His story was that he and Jannaeus, whom he had called out of ranks for an earlier breach of discipline, had been set upon by a band of rebel Jews. The soldier Jannaeus had been fatally wounded; he himself had narrowly escaped with his life. There were no witnesses. His word as a Roman officer was enough: Jannaeus, after all, had not even been a citizen.

The young officer would now take a detachment of picked warriors to scour the area for traces of the attacks. The hand of Rome would not leave them untouched. Sooner or later, the Jewish dogs would learn the true meaning of the word empire.

The hooves of the cavalry mounts clattered onto the baked turf of the parade area. Singly, and in pairs, horses and their helmeted riders shot from the dark stall openings as if catapulted from them. They formed four ranks and the young officer spurred his black mare to their head. Two giant men, moonlit drops of sweat like sewn pearls over their naked sinews, swung the gates open and the troop crashed out onto the flagstones of the square in front of the barracks.

They rode east and swung south at the city hall; they galloped past the dark, mastadonlike hulk of the Hippodrome. The moon and the overripe stars gave the Judean sky a ghostly luminescence; under this canopy, the rooftops of Jerusalem glowed with silver and lost themselves in shadows darker than the grave. Out beyond the city's walls, the surrounding hills sank ever more deeply into shadow.

The riders sped by the Pool of Siloam; they raced by the Rose Gardens, mysterious in their perfect silence and in their lacy patterns of light and shade. Nothing could seem more unearthly than the beauty of the earth.

They gained the road that led to the knoll. Puffs of pale dust burst beneath the hooves of the horses. The young officer used his spurs unsparingly on the mare. Behind him rode his men, who had been seized by his frenzy. They strained in their saddles; they slashed at their mounts; they bit their lips until blood flowed; they cursed into the immensity and stillness of the Judean wilderness; they thirsted to unleash their fury upon other men.

The young officer knew that he had infected them all. He goaded the mare to breakneck speed, to a pace he knew might burst her heart. He leaned forward into the night, his body rigid, his plume tossing wildly. His mind was icy with resolve.

TWENTY-SEVEN

The road passed through a clump of tall cacti whose spines trapped the moonlight at their tips and seemed to catch fire. Jesus walked on a carpet of needles as the road passed through a forest of delicate pines. He knew that he would soon reach the Valley of Kidron, that he would cross it, and from there ascend to the Garden of Gethsemane and the Mount of Olives.

He walked swiftly, shivering, and eventually folding his arms across his chest for warmth. Occasionally, he glanced back to see if he were being followed. He had made up his mind that he would not go back to them. They could turn him over to the Romans or kill him themselves or do whatever they wished, but it would not help them. He would never return.

A rabbit broke across the road and startled him. He stopped and watched it plunge into a thicket on the other side. It gave him a good feeling to stand and watch, and to feel that he was free to stand and watch. He wanted to be free to wander and to watch whatever he chose. Freedom made him feel invisible, made him feel he could go anywhere and watch anything. He felt closer to things than ever before. He felt that he understood.

He walked again. The moon was on the wane. It was weary and he could understand its weariness. Like a collapsing sail, it would yield to the winds of dawn. A chill edged into the air from the east. He shivered more strongly, but he did not mind. He saw things in a new light of freedom.

He walked and he understood the sighing of the pines: why should they not sigh? And when he reached it, he understood the desolation of the Kidron. Its rocks and boulders, their pale forms fading in the final hour before morning, reminded him of skulls. It seemed to him that a great host of skulls, human and animal, gazed at him as he moved along. He understood the blankness of their look. He felt that look within him at times: and he knew that one day it would be his everlasting possession.

The faces of his disciples appeared to him. Each face was a mask. He saw them standing together in a forlorn, uneasy group. Each figure seemed a mummy. By their bad faith and magical wishes, they were reduced to dead men in a common grave from which they would never arise. And they had desired that he die with them, so their deaths might not be disfigured by a stubborn life. He smiled sadly. They were a foolish, fanatic lot. But they would go down with this night. By the new dawn he would be rid of them.

His sandals struck the rocks resoundingly. He had almost crossed Kidron. Far in the distance, across an ocean of silence and space, came a harsh beat. Jesus recognized the muted thunder of Roman cavalry. These men of Rome were never quiet.

Now Jesus began the path upward. The road was of earth softer than that on the other side of the valley. Ahead, was Gethsemane and still higher the crest of the Mount of Olives. It seemed to Jesus that he was walking straight into the eye of the rising sun. Joy filled his heart: sureness and joy and a quiet peace. By the time he reached the cypresses of the Garden of Gethsemane, to which the last darkness of the night slung like spider-webbing, he was exhausted. He felt that he could go no farther and so he stretched out on the fragrant earth and fell instantly asleep.

TWENTY-EIGHT

The knocking sounded in his sleep. He was annoyed and he tried to smother it there. The old man's life was now closer to sleep and he did not like leaving it. But the knocking persisted. After a time, he opened his eyes and said, 'Who's there?'

At his side, the dog made an effort to come out of its stupor. The ghost of a growl formed in its throat and struggled to emerge, but in the end the animal gave up the attempt. An unfathomable dullness returned to its eyes. The door swung open. The dog paid no attention. Even the old man could not really stay interested. The small son of a neighbour stood in the doorway.

The child blinked and peered into the dim interior. His first glance went to the half-brother's pallet. He apparently was relieved to find it empty. He hated and feared the beady-eyed man with the long arms and cruel, deceptive fingers. But he saw then that the girl was also gone, and he was disappointed. He probably loved the girl; he could never tell her, or even himself, but it shone with painful intensity in his dark eyes.

'What is it?' said the old man hoarsely. 'What brings you here?'

The child hesitated and then said, 'My father says to tell you there is work for the Romans. He says to get ready; he will call for you in a little while.'

The old man grunted and the boy backed out, limping badly. He closed the door. The old man sat where he was, fighting the impulse to doze again. Yawning and muttering, he got up. He lit the oil lamp and then groped about for a crust of bread he had hidden some days ago. He found it after an irritating search and sucked on it with his gums. Then he located his sandals and laced them on with shaking fingers.

But his mind did not shake. It was fully awake now and tough as the hoof of a goat. A strange hunger fired it, as if it sensed that it must soon be extinguished. The old man paid little attention to the empty pallets. Only rarely did he think of his son and daughter, the surviving seed of his loins. He vaguely expected to be informed someday that the son had been found in a wayside ditch with a knife blade broken off in his chest, or that his daughter had been caught fornicating with a Temple priest and lashed half to death: the news would not have surprised him.

The forbidden bread was a pulpy mass in his mouth; his gums shifted it from side to side. He scratched his chest and armpits and loins and then drew on his cloak. He kept his tools in a worn leather pouch in the corner. Slinging it over his shoulder, he remembered other days, other jobs he had done, the strength of his arms and his back, women he had known in taverns and in the fields, the wine he had drunk, and the fights he had won.

Muttering again, he put out the lamp and walked to the door. Outside in the street, he breathed air that had in it the chill of approaching dawn. Soon the cocks would crow. He spat. Far off, there was the sound of a queer heartbeat: even his dulled hearing knew it for what it was – the heartbeat of death, the sound of Roman cavalry. He suddenly realized why he had been called to work. There would be holiday executions coming up and they needed him to work on the crosses.

TWENTY-NINE

She stumbled down the road, without knowing or caring where she went. Everything blurred before her eyes; a hum filled her ears. She was driven by her desire to leave the courtyard and the house and its master as she had left her own hearth, and by her resolve never to return, no matter what befell her. She had decided that she would rather go south into the desert with one of the madmen who claimed themselves prophets and healers than go back to her former existence. The freedom to choose her death was better than the living death of slavery.

Her initial pain and sense of loss diminished gradually. She did not give up her disappointment; it hardened to bitter hope. She felt she would meet the man whose face and eyes haunted her. Her vision cleared. She realized that she had been weeping, and she wiped away her tears. Her hearing became sharp. All of her instincts and the sum of her experience returned. The world was hard, especially for those who sought freedom, and she needed her wits and senses for what might come.

She passed through a clump of tall cacti that slowly, under the waning moon, retreated into their own shadows. They reminded her of Roman soldiers, bearing lances. She had to watch herself carefully: to fall into the hands of a patrol or ambush on a forsaken road in the early hours of morning was as good as death. But they would not, she knew, attack her without losing a man or two to her knife before they guessed what was happening.

A rabbit crossing the road alarmed her for an instant. It had emerged from a thicket on one side and dived into vines on the other. The sight of the small, innocent animal reassured her. Ahead, was a forest of pines. The silver in the needles of its trees was failing as the moon failed. It seemed to beckon to her and she entered it as if it were a mysterious chamber.

As she walked among the trees, she saw the face of her father. It was stern; the lips were clamped together; the chin quivered with rage. His eyes were blind and she knew he could not see her and so, she knew, the anger was within him. She felt pity, but she could do nothing to make the old man see, or to lessen his pain.

The faces of her friends and acquaintances slipped by, one following the other, like leaves. She saw the faces of neighbours, of those who had worked with her. Then she saw the face of the master of the house. It was bloated with drink; it was white, porous, already in decay. It floated like a rotting flower swiftly down the black river of her memory. And it was gone.

She saw the face of the lame child. She wondered if he knew that she understood his pain and the terrible pain of his love. She had known the boy from the day of his birth. She remembered the day on which he had been struck by the wheel of a passing Roman chariot and crippled. She remembered the screams of his mother, who had died not long after. She would miss only the child.

She walked among the stones of Kidron. In front of her, the shadows of jackals slid by. High above, the crest of the Mount of Olives lifted into trembling darkness.

She began her ascent and, inexplicably, remembered her dream of Gethsemane, the dream in which she had lost the one she sought without ever having found him. The she recalled the vision she had seen before the kitchen fire. This time, it was reversed. She removed his garments and knelt to the ground before him. She caressed his skin silently, and he submitted. He was tall and pale and his limbs, though strong, were thin. He gazed down at her as she touched him, but she could not read his look.

She reached the Garden of Gethsemane, but found that she was unable to continue. A terrible weariness had drugged her limbs. She sank to the earth, fighting the urge to close her eyes, but soon succumbed. She curled up on the accepting soil and slept within seconds. One hand clutched the handle of her knife.

THIRTY

Never in his life had he seen a purse fatter than the one he unstrapped from the sleeping torso of the master of the house. His fingers jiggled it out of nervousness and almost dropped it. When they caught hold of it securely at last, he pressed the greasy leather to his lips and kissed it. He wanted to scream out but restrained himself, though he knew his shouts would have aroused no one in that household.

Delirious, he held the purse closely to his chest. The wine roared through his mind like flames in an oven. He thought of a thousand things he would buy with the money, of a thousand women he would have, of a thousand enemies he would punish. He brandished a fist and giggled and choked back his giggling. Upon a sudden impulse, he staggered from the wall back to the table and picked up the carafe. His eyes blazed: he drank to victory. Wine soaked his neck and streamed inside his tunic, but he did not mind. What could annoy him on a night like this? He pulled the vessel from his lips, belched, and drank again. He would be a king on earth, a king of kings!

That sound again. His mind reeled. What sound? He held the carafe in one hand and clutched the edge of the table with the other. Was he certain he had really heard a sound? There was some signal in a far corner of his mind. If only he could decipher it. On a night like this, how could he listen to a signal he did not properly know was there? He drank again and grinned and shook his head from side to side. He saw a new life before him. He clucked his tongue. It would be as if he were reborn. He drank and wiped his mouth on his filthy sleeve.

The carafe fell from his fingers and smashed. Wine bubbled in the dust and faded at his feet. Of course he understood the sound. The beat of horses' hooves. He understood now. The sound of cavalry. He went pale with terror. The gate. He had to get out. But the sound was so close. He looked about wildly for a place to hide: the courtyard seemed naked. The house? He

68

was afraid to go in, trapped by the thief's fear of being trapped. His brain reeled. What could he tell them? What would they do to him? He saw the open gate again and lurched toward it, but it was too late.

The contingent of horsemen came crashing into the compound, striking sparks against the metal of the gate and boiling up clouds of dust. Simeon fell back, stunned, narrowly escaping the onrush of the lead mare, a coal-black animal with mad eyes and bloody foam gushing from her mouth. He stood in the yard, paralyzed with fright.

The young officer galloped to the far wall, swerved, and reined in his mare. She staggered under him, danced crazily back, and reared in the shock and pain of the abrupt restraint. Behind him, the cavalrymen divided into a great circle encompassing the entire courtyard. Their horses shook and stumbled. Their weapons clashed against shields and spurs. They fidgeted in their saddles and swore.

The officer sat erect, one hand grasping the reins, the other resting lightly on the handle of his sword. The only visible sign of fatigue was the ashen pallor of his skin. His eyes swept over the compound. He saw only two men who were awake: the idiot, who had risen from his pile of rags and straw as if from a coffin, and Simeon, whose terror had sent him, wringing his hands, in the other direction – to his knees.

'I recognize two of them,' called the officer. 'Place them under arrest – the vermin!'

His hand left the sword and itself became a sword. Two soldiers dismounted and approached the idiot. He shrank away and fell into a faint when they took hold of him. One cavalryman supported him under his armpits, spitting in disgust, while the other manacled his hands and feet. A third soldier brought a jackass from the stable and the idiot was flung easily across its spine. His feet dragged in the dust on one side of the donkey; on the other, flakes of straw fell from his tangled hair. Out of his pale lips a thick string of saliva rolled to the ground.

Simeon screamed when the soldiers came for him and the officer turned his mount so that he would not have to see the struggle that was certain to be an odious one. The boil on the back of his neck was throbbing unmercifully and he was annoyed with the mare. He pressed his lips together. His only satisfaction lay in the fact that he had so readily found those who would answer for the death of Jannaeus. Even this, however, did not cheer him when he thought about it for a moment. The young officer realized that the world was overstocked with victims.

THIRTY-ONE

He stood at her feet: a tall, shiningly metallic man outlined against the brightening disc of the sun. He was dust-covered; his sandals were worn and patched; a threadbare tunic hid most of his face. One of his arms was upraised and in its hand she saw a rock. She knew immediately that she would never be able to use her knife: he could smash her skull if she made any movement.

'How weary I am of metal men,' she said sadly.

The man's hand came slowly down; he threw the rock to the ground. He stood watching her without moving. She saw him clench and unclench his fingers.

'So am I,' he said hoarsely.

'Why did you threaten me with that rock?'

'I heard you come into the grove and did not know who you were,' he said. 'I meant to defend myself. . . .'

'Did you think at first that I was a Roman?'

'Yes.'

'Are the Romans after you?'

'They're after all of us.'

'I understand.'

'And they're not the only ones. . . .'

'I understand that also,' she said.

She sat up. The sky flamed and was melting to gold. Long steaks of blue curved through it like sandbars. Across the grey Valley of Kidron, Jerusalem looked as if it were on fire. The gold domes of the Temple seemed to be hurling their tiles back at the heavens; ten thousand rooftops gleamed; the walls of Herod's palace sparkled white as chalk. The air flashed like a mirror whose surface would never be stained with an image; through it, a flight of doves swirled, settling finally just inside the battlements by the Gate of the Essenes.

The man and the woman gazed down at the city in silence. After a time, she said:

'Have you watched me for long?'

'No.'

'Why did you stand there after you saw I was no threat?'

'Because you were so beautiful.'

'How do you know I am beautiful? Perhaps I only seem so?'

'Perhaps,' he said.

'And you? Your face is hidden by your garment. How do you look?'

'I do not really know,' said Jesus. 'I have never been able to see myself clearly. Up until this time, others have given me their picture of me and I have believed it.'

'Why do you say, "up until this time"? Is it different now?'

'I hope it will be different now.'

'In what manner?'

'I have left the city,' said Jesus. 'I am fleeing the Romans. And I am escaping them. . . .'

'Who are they?'

'Once, they were friends and comrades. Then they became captors and enemies. They are frightened men, that is the truth of it. They are frightened enough to believe in their own fears.'

'Are you a criminal?'

'Perhaps. I cannot tell.'

'A murderer?'

'If I have murdered any man, I have murdered myself.'

'That is not so. I do not see a dead man before me.'

'I was dead,' said Jesus. 'But I am risen from the grave. You see before you a man reborn.'

The girl was silent. She stared at the earth. Jesus sighed and said, 'And what about you?'

'I have fled the city as well.'

'From enemies?'

'From an old man who was neither friend nor enemy, who was nothing to me any longer. From his son who was my enemy and an even greater enemy to himself.' The girl looked up. 'I left nothing behind but the love of a crippled child, the son of a neighbour. But, in truth, I did not leave that, for I carry it with me wherever I go. Look into my eyes and you will see his pain and love. . . .'

'I have already looked and seen,' said Jesus.

'And I have looked into yours. They are strangely familiar. They remind me of someone I knew.'

'Who was this person?'

'A man,' said the girl.

'A lover?'

'I wanted him to be my lover.'

'What happened?'

'There wasn't time. I did not realize what I felt for him until I had left him. And when I returned to tell him how I felt, he was gone.'

'What sort of man was he?'

'I don't really know.'

'Then how do you know you loved him?'

'I know I do.'

'You can be certain?'

'I can dare to be wrong,' said the girl. She hesitated a moment and then she said, 'Let me see your face.'

She half-expected him to refuse. Instead, he reached up with one hand and quickly removed the tunic from his face. She gasped: it was the man who had been at the *Seder* table, the man she sought.

THIRTY-TWO

Still on his knees, Simeon screamed again as the soldier clutched his hair and pulled him by it to his feet. Sneering, a second soldier cocked back his arm and then dealt him a ferocious punch to the temple. The half-brother's head jerked back; blood squirted from his nose; his body flew through the air and bumped to the ground, rolling over and over in the dust of the yard. The first cavalryman stooped over and casually manacled him.

A third warrior led a nag up and the other two flung Simeon's limp body over its back. In the east, light blazed. The Mount of Olives stood forth as a brilliant cone of blue against the sky. Through the trees on its crest, the risen sun shot arrows of scarlet and gold. In the corner of the yard, a cock strutted out and crowed. A dishevelled band of servants crowded into the kitchen doorway; none would go any further.

The young officer dismounted and glanced idly in their direction. Holding to his sword, he said, 'Where is the master of this house?'

All of the servants pointed at once. Not one of them wanted to be left out.

'Rouse him,' said the officer.

The first cavalryman walked over and prodded the master's paunch with his boot. The round face, with its layers of fat, twitched comically and tiny bubbles of spittle formed on the thick lips, but the sleeper did not awaken. The soldier bent and dealt the man two ringing slaps on his soft cheeks and two yellow, uncomprehending eyes popped open instantly.

The master of the house was no fool. He sized up the situation immediately. A cousin had approached him with the idea of allowing a group of 'dissidents' to hold their *Seder* at his place. He had not liked the idea, but the cousin was persistent. The profit in it was first-rate: even the cousin's commission, when the master of the house recalculated it on the basis of the

74

obvious lie the cousin told him, was enormous. It was too fat a sum of money to pass up, especially in times when money was tight. The men who were making the *Seder* were not really rebels; they were babblers at most, men who fancied themselves heroes but were scared out of their wits at the first jingle of spurs. They raved, they ranted, they swung their arms like scythes and imagined they were transforming the world. They lived in constant dread of the authorities, but the authorities laughed at their kind. The Romans had more serious problems to contend with.

Apparently, he had been wrong. The middleman cousin had been wrong. He was safe in bed at home, sleeping on his money and dreaming of his whores, while he had to face the authorities. Yes, he had made a real error in his calculations; he hoped it was not a grave one. Brushing himself off, he rose to his feet, assumed as dignified expression as he could under the circumstances, and addressed himself to the youthful commander of the detachment.

'Your honour,' he called out, 'I am the master of this house; and may I tell you that you and your brave soldiers are welcome guests within its domain. I have nothing to hide from you. All is open to your inspection. I have done nothing wrong, committed no trespass against the laws of Rome, and so have nothing to fear from your unexpected but, nevertheless, pleasing visit. I am delighted to inform you that I will cooperate with you to the fullest so that you may expedite and conclude your business in the shortest time with the very least amount of trouble. I will help you obtain whatever it is you have come for—'

'Place him under arrest for harbouring the criminals,' said the officer.

'But your honour . . . everyone knows me . . . I am a loyal citizen . . . a respectable man . . . my reputation is well known in Jerusalem . . . you can ask anyone . . . my cousin knows the deputy commander of the—'

The flat of a cavalry broadsword brought the master's words to an abrupt end. Its blow broke his nose, shattered teeth into the trampled dust of the compound, blackened his eyes, and sheeted his big, shocked face with blood. He was manacled, bawling like a calf, and tossed across the nag's back beside the half-brother, Simeon. One of the maidservants cried out and a dozen hands clapped themselves over her face.

The officer turned and walked back to his mare. As he flung his leg over the salt-streaked flank of the horse, she faltered and collapsed under his weight, groaning with exhaustion. The officer sprang back. In a flash, before anyone knew what was happening, he drew his sword, rushed forward, and split the mare's skull like a melon with a single blow of the blade. Brain matter spattered in every direction, but the officer did not move, did not seem to notice that he was covered with gore. He stood as if in a trance while the soldier nearest to him came up and wiped him clean. Then, with a start, he seemed to come awake. He gruffly ordered the man away and began to clean his sword.

At his feet, the long legs of the slain mare jerked and twitched. Its rent skull glowed with welling blood like a pomegranate. Green-bodied flies buzzed over the carcass and began swarming on it before the spasms ceased. The reins and saddle were removed and two cavalrymen doubled up so that their commander could have a mount.

On his horse, the young officer gave the command to move. The detachment rode slowly through the gate, its weapons, shields, and ornaments shining in the light of the newly born day. Last of all in line came the donkey; it switched its tail and brayed loudly. Across the sharp ridge of its spine the rag-doll form of the idiot was doubled, wrapped snugly in the cloak of Jesus.

PART TWO

Pontius Pilate, Procurator of Judea, had not slept well. For the past few months, his bladder had been troubling him and its nagging pressure had forced him to get up three times during the night. The last time had been just before dawn and he had been determined not to succumb. But the discomfort had turned into pain and Pilate detested pain. Puffy-eyed, one cheek marked where the wrinkles in the bedding had imprinted themselves in its skin, he rolled slowly over, rose unwillingly and trudged to the toilet. Yawning and rubbing his chin he returned, relieved, to his bed. He sat on its edge, not even bothering to stretching himself out; he knew there wasn't a chance for him to drop off to sleep again.

The Procurator of Judea ran his fingers slowly through his shock of thick, greying hair. He was a tall, large-boned man in his late forties. His father, whom he had both admired and feared, had been a military man, a general-staff officer in a highly respected legion, and had seen service in many parts of the empire. Pilate, as a child and as an adolescent, had sometimes travelled with him, but had picked up little or no taste for the military life. He had been a quiet child and an aloof young man with an overriding passion for the precise arrangement of things. From his early years on, he had taken to collecting coins, minerals, seashells, plants, and even insects, which had first repelled him. He spent weeks and months gathering the objects for a collection and more weeks and months classifying and arranging them meticulously. He then would guard them jealously against the corrosion and ravages of the outside world. He felt safe with them and if anything ever happened to an object in a collection, he would fly into a rage and remain uncomforted for many days.

His awareness told Pilate that his craving for orderliness had led him into civil administration. In his youth, with excellent credentials and a modest fortune left to him by his father, he had risen steadily through the ranks. He was suave, shrewd enough to be able to affect shrewdness, capable of cruelty when he felt it was needed, debonair and possessed of a curious, almost diffident, charm. Those serving above him found him trustworthy and those serving under him found it possible to like him. He travelled through the empire and took pleasure in his posts.

Judea was another matter. It was the highest post he had obtained – it had cost him no small effort to obtain it – and the most troublesome. He found Judea an unearthly land; its uneasy people made him uneasy. Inside these Jews there burned an inscrutable flame: the more one flung water on it in order to eradicate it, the higher the fire seemed to jump.

Pilate was a man of imposing build and splendid appearance, but during the past several years lines of age had cut into his face and were beginning to change its entire character. For the first time in his long career, for the first time in his life, indeed, he was displeased with what he saw in the mirror. He understood the cause. Judea was doing it to him. Its blasted sun and its beastly people were ruining him, putting him into a coffin before his time. A spasm of pain went through his lower abdomen as he sat on his bed. He winced and touched the spot gently with his fingers. He was filled with disgust at the thought of illness. Tomorrow, he would consult one of the renowned Jewish physicians in the city. Judea attempted to cure what Judea attempted to destroy. He smiled bitterly. How delicate an irony! Too delicate, indeed, for a Roman.

Through the windows of his bedchamber, open to the spring night and soon to the new dawn, he heard the muffled sounds of the palace guards on their rounds. The grounds swarmed with them. He rubbed his chin anxiously. Agitation. Protest. Rebellion. War. Nothing kept to its appointed place in this insane country; nothing stayed where it belonged on the shelf. Searches. Roundups. Arrests. Trials. Executions. He liked his combatants placed where they were supposed to be: in an arena of sports. These crazy Jews wanted to make all of Judea an arena – what an outrageous idea! He toyed with the lobe of an ear. Well, if that was the way they wanted it, he could give it to

79

them that way. He had plenty of military men at his disposal who would be delighted to play games with them.

Wearily, the Procurator of Judea turned his head. On the other side of the bed was his newest mistress. Her breasts were exposed and he stared at them for some time. She was a beautiful woman and her breasts were full and yet remarkably firm for their size. Her dark hair spread over her pillow; the lids of her closed eyes fluttered. He wondered if she were dreaming and if it were so, what she dreamed. He had not felt well enough to touch her this night. Even now, he did not really want her. He only wanted to want her. His lack of desire worried him more than he cared to admit.

A rooster crowed. And then, farther away, another and still a third. A faint light flickered in the eastern sky. Soon he would be able to see the soldiers whose presence he had sensed through the night. His safety. His health. His love of life. His love of order. Judea interfered with them all. Bitter taste flushed into his mouth and he could not get rid of it.

THIRTY-FOUR

The old man and his young neighbour walked down the twisting streets of the city toward the main barracks, where the work was done. Because of the Passover holiday, few of the early risers were out. The morning was bright; even before the dew had dried, it was warm. The sky was without a cloud. In its bright depths, flocks of pigeons wheeled, each on its own, as if they did not belong to a common species. To the east, the mountains were clearly defined against the horizon; their flanks were ribbed with shades of blue and green.

The barracks were located on the western periphery of the city, not far from Herod's palace. Before the two men reached it, a beggar stepped suddenly out of a doorway and took them unawares.

'Let us pass,' said the neighbour.

But the beggar refused to give way. He was old, his hair was long and matted, his great, tangled beard was white but badly stained. Burrs and chaff were hooked into it. His lips trembled and his eyes shone, as if with fever.

'Abomination!' he cried out. 'Abomination . . . it's all about us! We are suffocating in it. We are drowning in it. We breathe the horror in with every breath we take. Our eyes are blinded by it. Our hearts are rotten with it. The monsters are in power and their monstrousness is everywhere about us. It is so pervasive that we have forgotten the way to live and begin to believe that their way is so. Their hideous images are everywhere and we forget that there are other images: our own. We sink, we plunge, into their monstrous schemes as into quicksand. We lose ourselves. We are destroyed. We cannot even remember that once we were men, good men, real men—'

'All right,' said the neighbour. 'We've heard your story. We've listened. We have nothing to give you, we're poor ourselves. Go to the rich, you scum. Get out of the way now and let us pass!'

The beggar did not move. His hand, thrusting out of a shredded sleeve like the hand of a skeleton out of a shroud, reached
up and plucked aimlessly at his filthy sore-covered face.

'Lackeys,' he croaked. 'Footstools! Mats on which the monsters wipe their bloody boots! Rags with which they clean the
gore from their hands! Don't you know they have poisoned the
air? Can't you understand that they are defiling that which is
best in you?'

'Get out of our way,' shouted the neighbour. 'We've got work
waiting for us.'

'Work? What work, you fools? The work of madmen and
predators! The work of a nightmare! Open your eyes and see
before they are gone. Open your hearts and understand before
you find you no longer have human hearts in your breasts!'

The neighbour stepped forward and shoved the beggar aside.
It scarcely took an effort: the beggar's body was only a husk, an
eggshell. It flew back and a dry, little exclamation of surprise
fell from his trembling lips like a withered pod.

'Jews,' he cried out, from the wall against which he had been
pushed. 'Do you dare to call yourselves Jews then? You are
nothing more than the dung forks of the Romans!'

The two men on their way to work at the barracks passed
him by. The neighbour cast his eyes down, but the old man
turned his head, looked the beggar straight in the eye, and spat
full in his face.

THIRTY-FIVE

Because she was the first to rise each morning and come down from her bedchamber at the first light of dawn, the servants in the palace thought she was crazy. She knew they did; she could see it in their eyes, but she didn't give a damn. After all, what did servants know? She smiled a crooked, malicious smile of whose existence she was scarcely conscious as she quickened her step down the broad flight of stairs.

The great reception hall was deserted. Beneath the row of enormous east windows, the marble floor was petalled with the rays of the morning sun. The light drew her there as if it were a magnet. Her bare feet picked up the delightful coolness of the ornately worked tiles. She stood quietly at the windows for some moments and then, pulling her blue-silk robe more tightly about her body, drew aside a translucent curtain.

She looked directly down on the royal gardens. In the centre of an immense lawn, a fountain fashioned of pink marble threw up a thin column of water that shattered like crystal high in the air. A dozen gardeners were already at work with rakes and short-handled hoes. In front of the great bank of rose bushes at the east wall of the palace, the guard was being changed; helmets and lances glittered. Beyond the walls, the streets would soon be filled with Jews in a holiday mood.

A queer, dreamy mood came over her, as if she had tumbled suddenly into a secret lake. She closed her eyes, and a familiar fantasy occupied her mind. She saw herself delivered by her husband, Herod, to the Jews. They brought her, wrists bound behind her back, to the public marketplace. There, her clothes were stripped from her: as each garment fell, a crier announced a sin she had committed. In the end, she stood naked before thousands of pairs of eyes. She was fearful and ashamed and, yet deep within herself, brazenly stimulated. She shook and cowered and yet her thighs were wet with the oil of her loins.

The crowd murmured excitedly as she was tied to a post. Two young religious Jews came forward and began lashing her over her back, buttocks, and legs with long, springy rods. The crowd sighed each time she was struck. She, too, cried out, but only because she believed it was what the crowd wanted to hear.

The pair of men kept whipping her until they were exhausted. Then another pair took their place. When, dripping with sweat and panting, they could no longer continue, the third pair began. She writhed and called out for mercy, but it was all pretense. It was merely to please the audience. For in the place of the pain she had expected, there was actually pleasure. Her nipples grew taut; her envelope swelled almost to the point of climax.

The performance waned. The last pair of floggers could scarcely wield their rods. The crowd became restless; some of the spectators drifted away. The sun set; it grew dark. The crowd thinned and, but for two or three vagrants, disappeared altogether. A torch was lit and a guard placed beneath it to keep watch over her. In the flickering light of the flame overhead, she examined her body. There was not a mark on it.

She leaned against the post, as fresh as when she had first been tied there, and out of the corner of her eye watched the guard devour her flesh with his eyes. He was very young, a mere stripling, and he feared her. She was abomination. After a time, he became drowsy, sat himself down on a bench and fell asleep, to do to her in his dreams what he could not do in waking life.

Just after midnight, two great archers from the main barracks passed by. Seeing her, they stopped. Their eyes glowed like embers; sparks seemed to flare in their nostrils. She twisted her hips and called out to them in a thick whisper. She gave utterance to the vilest thoughts she knew. She thrust out her breasts and cursed foully. Casting mad glances at her, they spoke between themselves and then, with incredible swiftness, sprang to the post, slashed her bonds, and bore her away to their post. She lay the night long on a mound of new straw in the centre of the parade yard of the barracks with her legs spread. In torchlight she was possessed by the entire complement of men quartered there.

From his place at a high window overlooking the yard, her husband Herod watched without stirring.

THIRTY-SIX

The stir on the parade ground – a bedlam of voices, the rapping of hooves, the jangling of weaponry, and the infernal braying of an ass – wakened Septimus from a dream of love. His brain whirled with its images; his enormous member was dark with blood and swollen with desire. He lay on his back for some moments, blinking with confusion: he could not understand how he had been suddenly robbed of the woman he was in the act of possessing. He had somehow been cheated, and his craggy face wore a look of puzzlement. He rubbed his eyes savagely, as if they were the ones betraying him, and then closed them again in an effort to recapture what he had lost. But he knew that he would fail.

His dream was strange. He dreamed that he was back in Rome again. It was a hot afternoon in summer and he sat with a group of friends in the great stadium, watching the gladiatorial contests. They had drunk much wine and their hearts were glad. A tall, powerful Ethiopian, new to the games, was fighting and they argued heatedly over his merits. They were carefree, ebullient, and flushed with the warmth of drink and friendship.

Suddenly, Septimus found himself transported to Judea. It happened in an instant, as if by magic. Rome vanished, the stadium and his comrades were gone, and he found himself in the beastly land of the Jews.

And there was yet another odd dislocation. He found himself once more in a stadium, but this time he was a gladiator, and the stands were filled with Jews looking on. He was not frightened, only bewildered by the transposition, and by the fact that he was standing stark naked on the sand and straw of the great ring without a weapon of any kind in his hand. Furthermore, there was no antagonist in sight anywhere. He stood and waited and still no opponent came forth, neither man nor beast nor monster. Sweating under the burning sun of Judea, watched by

86

the thousands of pairs of eyes encircling him, he became impatient and then angry. He lost all restraint, lifted his great arms, and cried out with all of his might: 'King of the Jews! Give me a weapon and I will slay whoever or whatever you may send out against me, be it man, animal or ghost! Or do not give me a weapon, if you choose. It does not matter a whit to me. I will slaughter my competitor with my bare hands!'

There was no response.

Septimus shaded his eyes against the sun. He squinted at the vast crowd of spectators, turning his head slowly and searching the stands. He could make out no royal box nor imperial guard. The great blisters of sweat on his flesh broke and rolled in thin streams down his arms, back, and legs; it spilled from his lips into his mouth, stinging like fire. He clenched his fists and screamed again, 'King of the Jews! Hear me!'

But his words fell only upon a formless mass of people. He could not understand. For the first time in his life, he felt lost. He gritted his teeth: somehow, the wily Jews had stolen his power from him. . . .

Then, from a hidden source, a voice called out to him: 'Fool! Roman jackass! The Jews have no king. They have only a queen. And she it is who will be your antagonist: the Queen of the Jews!'

At the far side of the stadium, a gate slid open. Through it a slim figure came. Septimus shaded his eyes again. He saw that his opponent was indeed a woman. She was tall, nearly as tall as he, strongly built, and also naked. She had black hair that fell almost to her knees and she laughed brazenly as she came toward him, as if to mock him as a man and a soldier.

He stared in utter disbelief. These Jewish swine were sending a woman against him, an unarmed woman. His rage overwhelmed him. He let out a terrible scream and rushed across the arena toward her. She neither slowed her pace nor turned aside in the face of his wrath. She smiled at him. Roaring, he flung himself over the final distance separating their bodies, seized her, threw her to the ground, and plunged down on her. Her thighs, breasts, and belly burned: though he wanted desperately to kill her, he realized he had instead penetrated her

87

and was locked in embrace with her. The crowd applauded thirstily to the rhythm of their intercourse.

He opened his eyes. The memory of the dream suddenly frightened him: he did not want to think of it any longer. He rose abruptly from his bed and strode naked across the barracks floor to the window. The other soldiers watched with awe as his massive frame passed. Some even closed their eyes and pretended to sleep.

When Septimus looked out, he understood what the fuss was all about. A cavalry detachment had brought in a group of rebel prisoners. He smiled wryly, yawned, and rubbed his immense, hairy belly with hands like paws. He knew there would be executions – work for him.

THIRTY-SEVEN

They stared at each other in silence and knew there was nothing more they could say until their bodies spoke a language neither had ever heard before. Their flesh had to speak for itself. They had cast a spell over themselves that only they could break.

The girl was on her knees, gazing up at Jesus' face. He bent and took her face between his hands and then himself knelt, keeping her face clasped between his palms. The pair was pale as apparitions among the roses and pomegranates of Gethsemane. The girl's lips parted and a small almost soundless word came forth, a whimper or a cry of triumph.

Jesus remembered that when he first saw her at the Passover table, he wondered to himself what would happen if he touched her. Now, through his fingers, her blood pulsed into him, and his own blood gave him the answer. She was so near to him that he saw her and yet did not. It seemed to him that she was a deep well, at the bottom of which he saw an image in the water, an image that was the reflection of neither of them. He wanted to cast himself into that well.

Instinctively they rose together. Jesus took her hand and led her up the mountain. He knew his way well, for he had often come here. He took her to a covert near the crest, and helped her through the thick screen of brush that surrounded it, using his own body to make way. Inside, they were alone, shut off from all. Only the sky, above them like a great overturned goblet scoured to incandescence by the unresting fingers of the sun, was witness to their wedding.

They removed their garments and lay together on the new green grass of spring. Their naked bodies touched. The call of a lark shivered across the last instant of restraint.

THIRTY-EIGHT

Peter wakened as the troop rode out of the yard. He saw the donkey, laden with the limp body wrapped in the cloak of Jesus, trot through the gate and disappear. All that remained was a cloud of yellow dust that shimmered in the morning light and vanished. He was so stricken with terror that it was a long time before he could think or move. When finally he managed to regain control over himself, he got up from the ground and rushed over to the table.

'They have taken Jesus,' he screamed, wringing his hands. 'The Romans have taken him prisoner and we are lost!'

The disciples awakened. Blinking, yawning, rubbing their eyes, they stared blearily at the man who stood where Jesus stood during the *Seder* service. He was pale, distraught, stunned.

'Do you realize what this means to us?' he cried brokenly. 'Do you know what will happen now? Have you any idea?'

No one answered him.

From the doorway of the kitchen, the mistress of the house, a stout woman with uncombed hair and a dishevelled nightdress, emerged and staggered uncertainly into the courtyard. She looked about her blindly and began to wail. A brood of terrified children clung to her legs and buried their weeping faces in her skirts. A group of maidservants crowded around them, trying to console their mother, telling her over and over again that she had no cause to worry. The more they tried to comfort her, the louder she wailed. Then with a final gasp of despair, she fell unconscious. Now the shrieks of the servants mingled with the higher cries of the children.

A few of the manservants went out into the yard and examined the carcass of the master's hound and the Roman officer's mare; they shouted contradictory orders at each other and quarrelled over several versions of what had occurred. They stamped their feet and beat away swarms of flies hovering over the fresh carrion. Two hardier fellows ventured out onto the knoll. They stood at the spot where the soldier Jannaeus had been slain and looked down silently at the bloodstained earth. The sound of a Roman funeral detail approaching frightened them away.

Peter was fully recovered by this time. He sat in the place of Jesus and scowled, trying to figure something out. His eyes were bloodshot; dark, ugly stubble covered his jowls; his over-sized jaw sagged. He picked at his teeth with a blade of straw, shifting his gaze from the servants milling around the yard to the vacant faces of the disciples at the table. He was filled with rage and impotence. He spat out the straw-sliver and said, 'They have taken Jesus prisoner and there can be no doubt about what will happen. He had no great love for us anyway; I'm sure I don't have to remind you of that. But now they have him in their hands. They will threaten him and he will spill his guts and tell them everything he knows. Our names ... our beliefs ... our religious ideas ... our hatred for the government ... our ideas about changing things. He'll deny his own part, I'm sure, and pin it all on us; yes, we'll take the full blame and get stuck with the punishment. He's a charmer: the Romans are certain to believe him and come looking for us. I don't have to give you any details about what that means. . . .'

The disciples stared at him like dumb oxen. Judas was on the verge of tears: 'Is there nothing we can do to save ourselves?'

'Perhaps,' said Peter, grimacing. 'Perhaps there is something we can do. But one thing we cannot do is remain in this place. We must withdraw to the desert at once. Get your things together and we'll leave.'

In haste they quit the courtyard without saying a word to anyone. As they left the knoll, they heard from the valley below the hollow-sounding dirge of the Roman funeral corps. Peter's knees shook and he quickened his step. The others followed suit.

THIRTY-NINE

Simeon regained consciousness in a small, low-ceilinged cell that stank of vomit and urine. He lay on his side on a dank, earthen floor which had drunk the tears and the blood of numberless prisoners. He lifted himself up on an elbow and peered into the dimness. He could make out two shapes that looked like sacks thrown down at random: the master of the house and the idiot. No sound or movement came from either.

He sank back on the floor and quietly groaned. His whole body ached. He feared that something might be broken or irreparably injured. He felt terrible thirst, as he had in his dream at home. Wearily, he licked the dry blood from his cracked lips. It tasted sweet. He closed his eyes and gave way to a numbness which stole over him.

There was a noise at the door. He froze. A hinge creaked. He opened one eye to a slit. The young officer who had given the commands in the courtyard walked into the cell. He was accompanied by a tall, thin, bald civil official in a dark uniform and by a deformed prison officer who carried a large ring of keys. The official stooped slightly and peered at each prisoner in turn. His bald head glistened; it looked like the naked bone of a skull. He cleared his throat and asked, 'These are the guilty parties?'

'They are,' replied the young officer.

'Are you certain?'

'I said so once. There is no need to repeat myself.'

'I'm just following official procedure; it has to be done.' The official smiled. 'That's what makes us civilized, you know.'

The young officer snorted. 'Those two,' he said, pointing a finger, 'were among the band that fell upon us. The other gave them shelter in his house.'

'I see,' said the official. 'Well, they'll get a quick trial, I can promise you that. It's the holiday season for these Jews and they sometimes tend to forget what's what in this country. A fresh crop of corpses might just drive a bit of sense through the heads of some of the fanatics.'

'They never seem to learn,' said the warden.

The other two ignored his remark. The young officer seemed preoccupied. He walked to where Simeon lay and prodded his ribs with his toe.

'This country is filthy with lice,' he said. 'They spread disease everywhere they crawl.' He dug his toe in more forcefully and the half-brother moaned. 'So ... you're alive, are you? Well, make the most of it, you pig, because you've not much left.'

The prisoner gazed upward. He struggled through the pain and fear to remember something he knew of this officer. Suddenly, he remembered.

'I know you, your honour,' he gasped.

'Damned effrontery,' snarled the warden, raising an inconspicuously carried truncheon.

'No,' said the young officer. 'Wait. Let me hear what he has to say. Perhaps he wants to give information.' He bent over and whispered to the battered face: 'Speak. Tell me how you know me. But keep your voice low if you wish to live.'

'My sister,' breathed the prisoner. 'I've seen you with her....'

The officer knew now who the man was. In spite of the pain in his neck, he bent still closer.

'What about your sister? I wish to know.'

'I know you do,' sighed the half-brother.

'What about her, swine?'

'Will you spare my life if I tell you?'

'Yes. But tell me quickly before I have a change of heart.'

'She has left,' the prisoner stammered. 'She has gone away.'

'Where has she gone?'

'The road to Gethsemane. I saw her go.'

The officer straightened up and kicked the man in the head.

'Jewish vermin,' he said, turning away.

FORTY

Though her eyes could not focus on him because he was so close to her, she saw him more clearly than ever before. Even when he was inside her, she felt that he had entered her in a way that had little to do with the responses of her flesh. It seemed almost as if she had created him, not out of the strength of her desire but out of the fullness of her love.

The weight of his body pressing her down made her feel light. In his possession, she felt his surrender. The gentler his caresses, the greater was his strength. Arms clasped around his neck, she gazed up past his cheek to the blue sky. A deep serenity came over her.

'I feel the peace of eternity,' she whispered.

'I know what you feel,' said Jesus, 'but that peace is a lie. It is not eternal at all; eternity is itself a lie. What you feel . . . what we feel . . . is deep and true. But it cannot last. And it will not.'

The girl knew he spoke the words as from within a cave. She knew that he, too, was at rest, that he drifted on a current which promised to sustain him forever. But she detected that a bitter light burned in his mind and refused to let him hide from what he knew. And she realized with satisfaction that he did not have to conceal himself from her, that he could show himself as he really was, and that she would accept him. The coupling of their bodies, at once so completely simple and totally unfathomable, as was always the case with the flesh, had shown them a vision of the world as soft and pliant. But the softness and pliancy of their love could not lessen by one jot their desire to face the sterner truths.

His arms were clasped about her waist and he gazed past her cheek at the sober countenance of the earth. They were both tranquil and filled with joy in the presence of each other as they lay within the shelter of the grotto. But the world crouched outside, waiting. She knew that they would have to fight for their lives as long as they were alive. Already, the song of the lark had ceased and the crows were cawing.

FORTY-ONE

The Roman quartermaster sat on a stool in a narrow strip of shade under the far wall of the barracks yard as he watched the crosses being built. He was a fat, lazy man with rumpled hair and a prominent nose that crawled with minute, inflamed blood vessels. He was a slow man, a man who walked and did everything slowly, a man who thought slowly, a man who was taciturn not out of discretion or reflection but simply because he did not want to use up the energy necessary for talking. He had drifted into the army in his early youth, had stayed not because he liked it but because he was too lazy to get himself out. Finding himself a suitable niche in it, he began the steady, slow job of fattening himself up. He sat and slowly chewed bits of dried carob which he occasionally bit off from a pod he gripped fiercely, as if someone might rush over to him suddenly and snatch it away.

He hated to expend energy on anything, including emotions, but this morning he could not prevent himself from being filled with disgust. He had been standing by when the funeral corps came in, marching at half-step and chanting the traditional dirge, and he had got a look at the body of the soldier Jannaeus they bore on a litter. He saw the torso and the neck stump, raw red and black with thickened blood. The severed head lay by it with the look of final terror stamped forever on its convulsed features. Over the remains a green haze of flies hummed stubbornly like a rasp on a piece of wood.

It had turned the quartermaster's stomach. He had nearly vomited.

He watched through narrowed eyes as a dozen hired hands worked on the crucifixes. He spat occasionally to indicate his profound disgust. His lips often twisted into an open sneer as he watched the workers. These Jews had no respect for anybody or anything. They ambushed, killed, mutilated. They did not even honour their own holidays. They were glum, shoddy workers and impossible people: obdurate, disputatious, carping, spiteful, and completely untrustworthy.

He grunted. It was an ill-conceived day that had ever brought him with his legion to this desert land of Jewish jackals. And then, on a rare impulse that surprised even himself, the quartermaster flung the pod at the nearest labourer.

FORTY-TWO

It hit the old man. He felt it glance off a shoulder, and out of the corner of his eye saw it skitter over the ground. The pod had not hurt him; it was only a slight, dry shell. He said nothing. He did not even glance over at the fat Roman who had thrown it. What could he care? He had received many a harder blow in his time and many a graver insult. As long as they paid him, what did it matter?

'I wonder why he did that,' said the neighbour.

The old man did not reply.

'We're probably not working fast enough for the fat son of a bitch. It's odd, though, he usually doesn't give a damn how slowly we work.'

The neighbour wiped the sweat from his brow. 'Unless they've got a lot of executions scheduled in the next day or two? That could be it. What do you think?'

The old man did not answer and did not bother to turn his head. He kept his eyes on the large cross of wood he was nailing together. It lay, looking bleached on the turf in front of him. He squinted at it, as if sizing it up before he put in the final nail. Except for the flies crawling on its surfaces and a heart-shaped single knot on the left side of the crossbar, it was flawless, as white as the flesh of a virgin.

'Do you think I'm right?' asked the neighbour.

The old man kept his mouth shut. He was being paid.

FORTY-THREE

The dry wind, the *khamsin*, blew over the face of the desert. The disciples huddled together in a tight circle. Their heads all but knocked and they drew their cloaks up over their mouths and noses. The wind came down on them and showered hot clouds of sand over their bent forms. It stirred the crests of the hills around them. Above them, the sky blazed like the uplifted shield of a warrior; in its fiery depths, a flock of buzzards circled heavily.

Peter's face grew dark. It looked like a tumour: only his eyes gave it semblance of humanity. He sat crosslegged, digging idly with a stick in the dust. No others moved or spoke. They seemed asleep, or inanimate. Peter glanced around the circle, broke the stick, flung the parts away, and spoke. 'We will have to disperse, my friends. We will have to pretend that we do not know each other, that we never have known each other. We must make it appear that we have never met . . . nor had dealings together . . . nor talked about government . . . nor discussed religion . . . nor planned to convert people to our ways and our beliefs.' He sighed deeply and continued. 'If any of us should, nevertheless, be caught and questioned by the Roman authorities, and if it should be shown that we had some acquaintance with Jesus, and if we should be confronted with the calumny he has spread about our lives and doings, then, my friends, we must hasten to call this Jesus a liar and a falsifier and a scurrilous traitor to the empire and emperor of Rome. In the strongest terms, we must denounce him as an enemy of Rome and a despiser of its people, customs, ways and gods . . . .

'We must show, my friends, how he is trying to place the guilt on us, how he is attempting to villify and slander and implicate innocent men, how he is out to avenge himself at random. We must make the authorities understand. And they will, my friends, if we are clever and persistent enough in our story, that Jesus will do anything to save his own skin. We can swear that we have seen him consorting with known rebels and turncoats, with murderers and traitors. . . .'

'Will not they ask us,' whispered Andrew, 'why we did not report the activities of Jesus to them, and why we did not turn Jesus in?'

'And we must answer,' said Peter, 'that he threatened us on our lives and the lives of our dear ones. We must say that it was only out of fear for the terrible revenge he would wreak that we kept our tongues silent. They will surely understand that. After all, the Romans are civilized men.'

The others nodded and bowed their heads. A hot blast of wind bore down on them and stung them with sharp pellets of sand.

'Roman justice will be done,' said Peter. 'The will of Rome shall prevail. Jesus will meet with the punishment and come to the end he deserves. Then the entire matter will blow over. Nobody will remember it. Nobody will distinguish it from a thousand other events just like it.

'How short, after all, are the memories of men. They cannot recall with any accuracy what happened an hour ago, let alone a day or week or month. The sands of time will cover each and every event and it is distorted and then buried altogether. All of history is as a howling wind. So the story of Jesus will be no more.'

'Will . . . will we ever meet again?' said Thomas, in a voice that trembled.

'We will meet again, one day. Yes, we will meet. It cannot fail,' said Peter.

'Who will lead us?' whispered Andrew.

'When the time comes, we will find a leader. Do not fear. Leaders can be found.'

'He must be the right sort of man,' said John.

'He will be the right sort,' answered Peter. 'I can promise you. I will find him and we will make him the right sort of man. We will shape him and mould him as we wish. He will not struggle against our will, as did Jesus!'

Judas lifted his head and sand ran down from the hood of his robe. Speaking slowly, in his heavy, low voice, he said, 'But suppose, in the confrontation of stories, suppose if we are caught and Jesus tells what he knows about us, what if—well, suppose the authorities believe him?'

'Idiot!' growled Peter. 'How could such a thing be possible?'

FORTY-FOUR

The grand chamber of the Procurator of Judea with its lofty, domed ceiling, its splendid mosaic floor, and niched busts of marble, was kept as silent as possible. The dome grasped even the slightest sound and lifted upward in a spiral, whirling it back to the floor below. If voices were not well modulated and strictly controlled, the room could become a chamber of wild cacophony.

It was common knowledge among his aides and servants that Pontius Pilate preferred modulation to excitement and silence to modulation. In a hushed room, the Procurator felt composed, certain, adequate to every task and any eventuality. Noise confused, irritated, and frustrated him: it vitiated his judgmental powers and mental acumen.

Following his usual warm bath and a leisurely breakfast, the Procurator relaxed at his great table, one elbow resting lightly on its green marble top. He listened with interest and even a certain kind of pleasure to the words of a trusted aide, a venerable, grey-bearded fellow who had served with him for many years and had known his father before him. The man spoke slowly and eloquently, scarcely lifting his voice above a whisper. He laced his report with wit and the latest gossip. Nearby, a scribe sat and waited patiently for anything that needed to be recorded. Pilate felt that the uneasiness and discomfort of the night had abated. In the calm, considered, austere orderliness of familiar surroundings, the Procurator felt quiet elation. He felt assured that nothing ever would or could depart from the fixed patterns he had set. Here, he was eminently capable of keeping life strictly within an arena of his own choosing where it could run smoothly. Pilate was not afraid to admit to himself that he despised life's dark corners and dirty back rooms.

He listened, but his attention began to wane. He crossed his legs, removed his elbow from the table, and folded his hands loosely on his knee. A large, gold signet ring shone up at him with a friendly glint. The aide droned on: tax revisions, a land dispute between two of the wealthiest Jews in the city, a new edict from Rome on religious observances among subject peoples, the arrival of a legation from Damascus, plans for a party in honour of the departure for home of the general of a resident legion. The aide's voice purred, soothed, flowed forward with the cheerfulness of a brook. Pilate nodded occasionally to show that he was attending, but he actually permitted his mind to wander more and more. He trusted the stability and shrewdness of the aide, as manifested in the singular harmony of his voice, to carry him safely to the proper conclusions. When the report ended, Pilate would request a summation and recommendations for action. Subsequently, he would dictate his orders to the scribe. He then would receive official visitors and petitioners. The smooth machinery of civilization would spin flawlessly throughout the day.

There was a stir at the doorway. Pilate had tried to ignore it for some time, making an effort to concentrate on what the aide was saying in order to disregard it. He loathed interruptions. After a time, though, the aide felt compelled to halt his remarks and turn to the direction of the imposition. Annoyed and upset as he was, Pilate could not help himself: he was forced at last to follow the aide's gaze. Slowly, he turned his well-chiselled neck, shifting the weight of his entire body and arching an eyebrow in disdain. The fingers of his left hand gently sought out and stroked his ring.

The Procurator saw the admissions officer, flanked by two of his personal guards, wrangling with a man he recognized as the deputy military commander of the city. Pilate appreciated the fact that his admissions officer respected to the letter of the law his superior's wish for decorum and protocol, and he greatly valued the officer's zeal in carrying out orders. A visit from the deputy city commander, as unexpected and incursive as it was, could definitely not be turned aside with impunity. There were unwritten laws with which the custodian of the door was not familiar. There was no choice: the uninvited visitor had to be admitted. Frowning, the Procurator beckoned his aide closer and issued instructions in his muted baritone.

The aide hurried across the great chamber, reaching his destination quickly, even though he limped badly.

The parley began and Pilate shut his eyes. He saw the nude body of his mistress in bed. He saw her dark hair spread over the pillow, the white curve of her neck, the thick tautness of her nipples. The desire which he had missed so sorely during the night was upon him. He wished himself in bed with her at that instant. He stifled a sigh and opened his eyes. The aide was escorting the military man up to his table, trying desperately to keep pace with the soldier's rapid stride.

'Well,' said Pilate, forcing the muscles of his face into a cheerful smile. 'Well, my friend, what brings you to me at such an early hour of the day?'

The officer was a big, sleepy-eyed man, with a pale complexion and a heavy jaw, which he continually rubbed. He did not smile in return, but simply saluted properly.

'Your Excellency,' he declared bluntly, 'I bear no good tidings. I am here to inform you that there has been another attack by rebel forces on our men. We have lost a man, a good soldier of the empire; and we very nearly lost one of our best young officers. Only a miracle saved his life. I am here to convey to you the strong and urgent desire of the commander of the city of Jerusalem to respond quickly to this outrage. Something must be done today.'

'On a holiday? Are you mad? Has the Judean sun gone to your heads?'

'Even the slightest delay, Your Excellency, must only be interpreted by the enemy as a sign of weakness on our part. Weakness encourages them; strength deters, Your Excellency. Weakness hesitates before it acts; power speaks on the instant. We have no choice. We cannot turn our eyes away from the slaughter of our troops in our own midst.'

'A trial on a holiday? Impossible. I find it difficult to conceive of such a thing. Tell me, are you certain it must be so?'

'Not only a trial,' said the officer, rubbing his chin and moving his heavy jaw deliberately, as if he were chewing sentences up into words, 'but a trial and an execution. Promptly. Today. The city commander insists on this, Your Excellency.'

'Insists?' repeated Pilate, glancing at his aide as if expecting help from him. 'The city commander insists?'

'That is correct, Your Excellency. Those were his exact words and he made it a point that I should repeat them as he spoke them to me. Otherwise, he begs to inform you that he cannot be held responsible for the security of this city and the safety of the Roman officials who dwell here. He is willing to go on record in this regard, Your Excellency, directly to Rome. This, Your Excellency, he instructed me to convey to you in precise terms as well, so that there may be no mis-understanding.'

The Procurator winced. He put his ring finger to his pursed lips and considered: correspondence directly to Rome, the city commander, a trial, executions, holidays. So the Jewish gadfly was stinging him once again. Well, then he had no choice but to swat it and to swat hard. He bit the finger gently and reflected for some seconds in the blissful silence that returned to the chamber.

'Perhaps you're right,' he said in a low voice, almost as if he were musing. He dropped the finger and sat up. 'Very well. You may inform the city commander that I have decided that there will be a trial of these rebels this very afternoon and that exe-cution of the criminals will take place directly following it. I presume that you have the guilty parties securely in your cus-tody. . . .'

'We do, Your Excellency. Three of them.'

'Splendid!' Pilate smiled. 'Three of them, you say? Well, there will be three less come evening.'

The officer saluted, turned, and left briskly. The Procurator sat and watched him quit the chamber. His face became gloomy, even mournful. The symmetry of his morning had been rudely destroyed. His entire day was off-balance. There would have to be preparations for the trial. Already, with the officer barely gone from the room, his aide looked up at him for instructions. Out of the corner of his eye, he saw the scribe lift his head attentively. A pain shot through Pilate's lower abdo-men.

The Jewish gadfly again.

FORTY-FIVE

Septimus was made restless by the strange dream, followed by the sight of prisoners being brought in. He immediately went in search of Gregorius, a brawny infantryman and the only other soldier on the post who was anywhere near his own size. He persuaded him to get out of bed and wrestle with him. The two men went directly to a corner of the yard reserved for the purpose, drawing onlookers as they walked. Soon a large crowd was gathered as word spread quickly of the contest. Bets were made. Whistles and curses filled the air. These opponents always drew the biggest crowds and the largest bets, for they were giants and skilled in wrestling. Stripped to loincloths, they began circling each other, hunching their shoulders, feinting, moistening their lips with their tongues. Their muscles rippled and their bronzed flesh glistened in the morning light. The number of spectators increased. Several noncommissioned officers were in the crowd, and there was even a commissioned officer with a small, pinched face and drooping shoulders who had slipped in unnoticed. There was a special fascination for the soldiers when the executioner, Septimus, fought: it was like watching the angel of death.

Septimus and Gregorius had wrestled many times before. One did not consistently better the other. They were about evenly matched as combatants. But today Septimus felt strange. He felt that he had to win and he was determined to do it. A painful fire burned in his chest; something within him needed release. The very sight of his opponent annoyed him. The shouts of the crowd irritated him. He had the queer feeling that he was reenacting his dream, even though he plainly knew he was awake and knew exactly where he was. For his part, Gregorius was unsuspecting. He was as always good-natured, easygoing, cheerful, always ready to accommodate a friend if he could. He was out to enjoy a good morning's exercise.

Gregorius had muffed the first opportunity. Still not fully awake, he moved sluggishly and Septimus slid away from his grasping fingers. The crowd sighed and moved back slightly as the dust rose into the air. Gregorius also had the next chance. This time he did grasp Septimus, but the latter broke the hold easily and sprang back. The crowd moaned, ignited by something subtle in the executioner's mood. One voice rang out. It belonged to a thin, bandy-legged soldier with a shock of flaming red hair. He was known as Wasp and his harsh, derisive voice grated on Septimus' nerves.

The next opportunity was his. He took advantage of it and trapped Gregorius in a headlock. Contact with his opponent's body filled him with a red burst of rage, and he tightened the hold. The combatants crashed to the ground and rolled over in the dust. Septimus exerted his enormous strength. The sense of his dream maddened him. The crowd roared. The little soldier nicknamed Wasp hopped from one foot to the other and foamed at the mouth. Terrible sounds issued from Gregorius' throat. His legs thrashed helplessly about. His eyes bulged from their sockets. His giant's frame went suddenly, absurdly limp.

The executioner might have killed his opponent had it not been for a group of onlookers who realized what was happening and pulled him away. Great bands of sweat ran down his face and body. His breath came in gasps. He looked as if he were in shock. Eight men kept him from moving back to the fray. Gregorius was unconscious, but there was yet life in him. Several men bent over his inert form. At last, he began to revive, crying out weakly like a child.

Septimus turned away. He left the yard without a word to anyone. He had a bath and ate a huge breakfast and then headed for the brothel. It was not open in the morning, but with cursing and threatening he bullied his way in. No one really cared to argue with the executioner. Septimus pulled a tall, new girl out of the bath. He led her naked down the hall. Her wet feet made a track directly to the bed. He looked at her long, black hair, and her swarthy complexion. There was a faintly mocking smile on her lips.

She looked remarkably like the Queen of the Jews in his dream.

FORTY-SIX

The young officer rode slowly through the dewy greenness of Gethsemane. He had not slept in nearly forty hours. But he did not feel weary. He seemed not to know that weariness existed. He recognized only the terrible insistence of his pursuit.

He did not appear to be in a hurry. He did not urge his mount on. Something told him he would find his quarry. He rode steadily, patiently. His roan stallion picked its way nervously up the slope, but the Roman officer astride its back was not nervous. He was perfectly calm. His eyes and ears were ready to catch the slightest sign of his prey.

The soldier Jannaeus had sought to thwart his will and he had paid Jannaeus out. The girl had frustrated him, but he had been patient for a time. Time was running out and his forbearance ending. She would taste the bitter consequences.

Away from Gethsemane, he had a clear view. Within moments he caught sight of the girl. She was in the company of a man. They walked slowly, held hands, and were smiling at each other. The meaning was plain. Almost at that instant, they saw him and halted.

The young officer did not need to calculate. The machine of his mind was always in motion and commanded his body. He dug his spurs into the stallion's flanks. He slashed the reins across its neck with one hand and with the other drew his sword. Scarcely a hundred yards separated him from the couple. They had no protection to look toward, not even a bush on this bare stretch of slope. Sword high in the air, he thundered toward them.

But in the final ten yards of the ascent, the horse, highly strung and terrified by the strange rider and his abuse, missed footing and spilled the officer to the ground. His head struck a rock. He lay unconscious.

FORTY-SEVEN

The completed crucifixes were stacked neatly against a wall of the yard. Their black and dense shadows lay on the pale white expanse of the turf. Carrying his tools, the old man passed through the shadows without paying the slightest apparent attention. If he thought anything at all, it did not show in his wizened face or in his dulled eyes. He walked slowly over to where the quartermaster stood and was paid his wages. He received three coins, which he folded carefully away in his cloak next to his flesh.

The neighbour had not waited for him and the old man trudged homeward by himself. He walked through holiday crowds, but he paid not the slightest attention to them. Since early morning, he had eaten nothing, but he was not in the least hungry. Somehow, with each step he took, his feet seemed to get heavier, to drag more. Clutching his tools, he forced himself on.

Something lurked in a dark corner of his consciousness, but he could not say what it was. The hidden thought nagged at him and he tried to ferret it out, but he had no success. As he drew near his house at the end of the narrow cul-de-sac, he felt his knees weaken. His breath grew short as if someone meant to deny it to him. In front of his door, the crippled boy waited. His large eyes shone with pain.

'Where is the girl?' the child asked.

The old man stopped. He scarcely heard the question, or understood that he was being addressed. There were no ghosts of past wives and children in his mind. There was only the painful awareness of something hiding from him, the thought that oppressed him.

'Where did she go?' the child's quavering voice asked.

The old man brushed past the boy. His fingers struggled with the latch and then he had to use all of his strength to get the door open. It had never in his life seemed so heavy. The boy was wailing in the street and he shut the door on his sobs. He saw the dog's dark, stiff shape on the floor and knew the meaning of it. He knew also that something far beyond the animal's death was wrong.

As water seeps through clay, an eerie feeling came over him: it stole over his limbs and then closed in around his heart. His tools fell from his hand. The child's voice through the door sounded as if it came from the distant desert. Very little breath was left now. He became dizzy. Darkness struck his eyelids. In the growing darkness, the black thought he had sought so assiduously grew at last clear to him: it told him that he was going to die. Every portion of his body whispered a part of this truth to him until it was a roar that filled his mind. He had time to feel nothing. The thought was swift, final.

The body fell lifeless beside the carcass of the dog with its distended belly and frozen eyes. It lay with arms outstretched on the floor as if it was nailed to one of the crosses made that day. The old man lay on his cheek. The earth he had trodden stuffed his mouth.

FORTY-EIGHT

Peter lifted his arms and stared past them into the brittle blue glass of the desert sky. He wanted to smash it and so destroy the world. He had dispersed the other disciples, bumbling idiots that they were. He remained alone, for he had sickened of their calf eyes, slack jaws, trembling fingers, and jellied spines. He was weary unto death of their whining and caterwauling. Alone, he could brood in peace and taste his bitterness to its core. He dropped his arms despondently as if they were the branches of a dead tree. He closed his eyes, but the glare of the sun persisted on his retinas.

His despair was bottomless. All of his hopes and plans to create a following, a movement, a tidal wave of humanity which would sweep the world as it was away forever had been dashed. Whatever headway he had made had vanished in a flash. The very man he had chosen and groomed as a figurehead had been snatched from him and, furthermore, would be made to give evidence against him.

He could see Jesus on his knees before the Roman interrogators, babbling spittle in his haste to incriminate the lot of his former comrades. He could hear Jesus plead for his life and could feel the terror rise from his flesh like the fierce odour of a wild beast. He realized that he hated Jesus more than any other man.

Eyes shut tightly, he prayed in hatred to some infernal spirit. He was in a trance; his fingers clawed the sand; his lips twisted convulsively; his body shook. He saw Jesus flogged, hung, drawn and quartered, pierced by a rain of arrows. He saw Jesus on a crucifix with nails through his wrists and ankles.

This last vision appealed to Peter more than all others. He liked the idea of imposing a slow death on a prisoner, a death that both victim and executioner had time to linger over and savour. He liked the manner in which, on the cross, the body was frontally exposed, so that its shame and hurt were revealed to all eyes. He admired the way in which the arms of a crucified man were pinioned back, as if the executioner were saying over and over to him, 'See how utterly helpless you are and how absolutely we have you in our power!' Peter shuddered with loathing. He felt that he would gladly have driven the spikes into Jesus' flesh. From the start, the man had been a disappointment to him. Now he was a disaster.

Peter was roused from his fantasy by an odd noise, like the whirring of bees. He opened his eyes. In the distance, a great throng of people was passing. The people had come from the city and were heading into the desert. There were beggars of Jerusalem, the hunch-backed, the blind clinging to the rags of those in front of them, the lame, epileptics foaming at the mouth and rolling their eyes, the deaf with their hands spidering into the air above their heads, the disfigured, the insane, the maimed, the living dead, cripples dragging their broken bodies over the earth like worms. A shaggy, hulking mute led them. He gazed upwards, shaking his fists at some phantom or vision and shrieking voicelessly. A cloud of dust boiled over the heads of the mob. Far up in the cauldron of the sky, vultures circled patiently for a feast that was certain to come their way.

Peter was terrified. He bent over to the ground and slowly began to back off from the prophet and his host, sliding like a crab. When he was far enough away, he rose, and ran as fast as he could until he was over a hill and completely cut off from their view. Even that was not enough. Dripping with sweat and covered with sand, panting, shaking from head to foot, he crawled into a clump of cacti and threw himself onto his back. He stared up at the tall green columns whose cruel white spines reminded him of the spikes he envisioned for the body of Jesus, the informer and betrayer. His body was numb with exhaustion, but his hate seemed to burn on an inexhaustible fuel. He lay motionless, looking up, for a long time until he fell asleep.

FORTY-NINE

He saw only shadows. Perhaps, he thought through his pain, he had passed into the land of the dead, the land of ghostly ancestors and slain warriors. Gradually his vision began to clear, and he finally saw that two people were standing over him. One was the girl he sought and the other the strange man in whose company he had last seen her. He could hear the roan stallion moving about, but the animal was out of his range of sight.

The girl stared down at him. It was obvious, from the expression on her face, that she recognized him. The man, some sort of Jewish ragamuffin, brandished a rock. His long, sad, Jewish face was filled with wrath. The girl reached out and stayed Jesus' upraised arm.

'I know him,' she said.

'What does that matter?'

'Perhaps you're right. Perhaps it doesn't matter a bit. But why do you have to kill him?'

'Because he wanted to kill us. To ride us down and slaughter us in cold blood.'

'He's powerless now. He can't move a muscle. I think he's broken his back. What harm can he do us?'

'The very sight of him sickens me. He's a poisonous snake.'

'He can't do a thing to us. Don't you see?'

Jesus stared at the girl. 'Maybe you're right,' he said softly.

The girl gently touched his cheek. A weary, haunted look came over his features. He sighed deeply and threw the rock aside. Then he bent and leaned over the young officer. 'Can you speak at all?' Jesus asked.

The officer thought he could speak, but he did not want to try. Let them think he was dumb. He did not wish to be questioned when he was at the mercy of his interrogators. He stared up with a steady, unblinking gaze, and said nothing.

'Can you hear me?' asked Jesus.

The young officer did not reply.

'We cannot remain here,' said Jesus, straightening up and turning to the girl. 'They'll be out in force looking for him, you can be sure of that.'

She nodded. 'All right. Whatever you say. . . . Shall we take the horse? It doesn't look injured.'

'Yes.'

As severe as was the pain in the young officer's body, it was still more intense in his mind. Only the hope of vengeance pulled his mind through its ordeal. Compelled to lie helpless, he was unable to do anything or to issue the command for others to do something, while enemies mounted the stallion that had betrayed and almost killed him. Had the power been his, he would have ordered the animal slain even before the humans, so fierce was his hatred of it. All three would have perished within minutes and all three carcasses would have been flung to the beasts of the fields.

He lay without moving, as he heard the couple mount the horse and then heard the animal's hoofbeats fade slowly away. Only the chirping of birds and the humming of insects remained. When the young officer was absolutely certain his enemies were out of earshot, he opened his mouth and screamed with pain.

FIFTY

Simeon dreamed that his half-sister was a real sister, born of the same parents as he, and that the two of them were to be married. Somehow, the priests had turned their eyes away and would permit the illegal union to take place. The half-brother was overjoyed.

The wedding was magnificent. It took place in a splendidly appointed hall, decorated with great banks of roses and gladioli, and graced with singers and scores of musicians. There were numberless tables laden with food and drink. The bride wore a robe whiter than the snow of Mount Hermon's peak. Fresh lilies were woven into the tresses of her jet-black hair. All of the dignitaries and elders of the community were there. Even Herod, king of the Jews, and members of the royal family attended. The Roman hierarchy was also represented. Pontius Pilate had fallen ill that day, but had sent a special envoy bearing his most profound apologies and a gift of dazzling jewels.

The bridegroom was flushed with pride and pleasure. He revelled in the pomp of the ceremony, which was performed by the high priests of the Temple itself in the munificence of the feast, in the sumptuousness of the decor, in the brilliance of the guests, in the beauty of the music, in the incredible deluge of gifts showered on the nuptials. His greatest adoration was concealed deep within him, for it was for his beloved bride. He longed to draw the veil from her face, to kiss her lips again and again. Unable to bear restraint any longer, he would take her virginity, and he would possess her the night long. He became weary of the great mob of guests who pressed forward, wave upon wave, to offer noisy congratulations. He began to be bored with the endless repetition of the toasts and the vulgarity of the jokes. He was sated with the wines and sweetmeats, the pastries and puddings. From all eyes he hid the overwhelming desire to be alone at last with his new wife in their marriage chamber.

Eventually, in the early hours of the morning, when scarcely any time at all remained before the coming of the dawn, the final few guests departed for home. Simeon, utterly exhausted, sustained only by his desire to unite carnally with his cherished bride, led her to their secluded room and locked the door behind them. There was no need to light a candle for the light of morning flared already in the east. With trembling fingers, he turned back the white satin cover on the great bed. Then he faced his bride, who stood waiting meekly, silently, with her slender arms at her sides, and drew aside the veil.

He was frozen with horror. Instead of the visage of the beautiful woman he knew and desired, there was the ravaged face of a corpse. Inside the sockets of the rotted eyes, among shreds of black cadaverous flesh, maggots squirmed. Mouthless, the face yet laughed at him. . . .

Drenched with sweat and blood, he wakened with a scream. From the other side of the cell, a voice called out to him. 'What's the matter over there?'

'Who are you?' whispered the half-brother.

'I am a respected citizen of Jerusalem. And you? Who are you?'

Simeon told him. There was silence. Then the master of the house asked, 'Why did you cry out?'

'I had a dream,' the half-brother said through chattering teeth.

'What about?'

'I dreamed of death.'

'That was no dream, my friend,' said the master of the house. 'That was the truth.'

'They will kill us?' choked Simeon.

'We will surely die,' replied the master of the house.

'We will die? Why? What reason?'

'There is no reason. They have decreed it, and that is all the reason they need.'

'But I do not want to die. I tell you that I do not want it.'

'Still, you must. And so must I. And the third one who is with us, though I know not his name nor what manner of man he may be, he, too, must perish.'

'I will not die,' whispered Simeon. 'I say to you that I will not die. I cannot do it.'

Sprawled on the dung and the straw of the dark cell, he burst into tears. And his tears mingled with the blood and grime caked on his face and with the sweat that gushed forth from his pores. He wept brokenly with no more voice than a dog. The master of the house wept with him. Alone, the idiot was silent.

FIFTY-ONE

She breakfasted alone. Only the soft footfalls, and occasionally the hushed voices of the servants, disturbed the profound silence of the dining hall. Her mood was surly and bitter. Her food tasted flat and she pushed part of it away. She snarled at the men and women who waited on her. She felt exhausted, as if she had not slept that night. By the time she rose from the table, her eyes shone with sullen anger.

Her bath was protracted; that was why she preferred eating first. Bathing was usually a sort of adventure for her. Three or four specially selected young attendants soaped her, laved her, dried her with great care and gentleness, and oiled her limbs and the rest of her body as if they were priestesses anointing a goddess. They went through all of the ritual stages this morning, but the experience did not change her mood.

Standing in front of a huge, round mirror framed in silver filigree, she gazed at the reflection of her nude figure and the sight was distasteful to her. The reflections of the young lithe forms of the nymphs who served her, themselves almost naked as well, did not, as they often did, arouse her. She viewed them also with distaste. Sometimes, for added stimulation, there were adolescent males in attendance as well: today, she did not allow them in. The fantasies of the bath bored her; they were stale.

Dressed, she returned to her bedchamber and stood by the window. She had fixed an appointment with a lover, one of several young court fops whom she cultivated for that purpose, as one cultivates animals for amusement. When she heard his knock at her door, she did not open it. The gentle knocking persisted and she ground her teeth. Finally, her patience strained, she hurled vile phrases at the door. There was abrupt silence. The caller knew full well that one did not tamper with the moods of Herod's wife.

She stood and stared moodily out of the window. She stifled

a yawn. Then she rang and requested a court singer. He came immediately. He was a fair-haired young man with a fine tenor voice who accompanied himself skilfully on the lute. She tired of him almost before he had finished his first song. Her look was sufficient to dismiss him.

Idly, she wondered where her husband was. Quarrelling with him was sometimes sport. That was no real outlet. It, too, had lost its former charm. When a maid-servant entered the room through a private entrance, she whirled suddenly and struck the girl across the face. When the maid dared to cry out in pain, she struck her a second time and summoned the head maid, ordering her to dismiss the weeping servant from her staff, though she was one of the most gracious and efficient of the lot and an open favourite of long standing.

Alone, again sullen, she quit the bedchamber and on an impulse went up to the palace roof. There were many sections of the vast expanse: gardens and alcoves and nooks, patios and grottos, places for every design of the mind and purpose of the heart. She walked aimlessly, muttering under her breath, and finally ascended to the highest rampart, where four handpicked palace guards, brilliantly arrayed in purple and silver, kept watch at their posts.

She held to the railing and gazed outward. The sky was cloudless. Beyond the walls of the city, the fields and meadows were radiant. Through the distant hills wound the roads that went to Gaza and Bethlehem. To her right, the Serpent's Pool flashed like a mirror. Directly before her eyes, on a green sward atop a knoll, was the Herod Family tomb. The very sight of it depressed her. She knew that one day she must be sealed within its marble walls, a feast for the family of worms whose generations lived on Herod's ancestors. She averted her eyes quickly to the left, shading them against the sun. Her gaze was drawn to the hill of Golgotha, on which some sort of activity was taking place, outside the city wall. She squinted and made out soldiers and workers erecting crucifixes.

She watched the preparations carefully. A strange dryness came into her mouth. Her heart pounded painfully. There would be executions. She would inquire, find out when they were going to be held, and attend. She could scarcely wait.

FIFTY-TWO

The swarthy, dark-haired prostitute lay on the soiled bed. Black-and-blue marks covered her body. Her lips were swollen and torn; her thighs were bruised; her insides were ripped. She rolled over and sobbed bitterly to the wall. The madam and several of the other girls tried to comfort her, but she pushed them away as if to say they could flog her or starve her or even kill her, but she would never lie with Septimus again.

Septimus was well satisfied. The dark-haired girl, whom he had never seen before and who must have arrived in the brothel within the past few days, had given him considerable pleasure. It was true that larger breasts and more fleshy buttocks would have better suited his taste, but he had nothing to complain about. The girl had thrashed about with her long, shapely legs, had pummelled him with her fists, bitten and clawed and cried out many times during their intercourse. This had greatly excited him and when spent, he felt immensely relieved. Somehow, he was at last freed of the dream and its puzzling aftermath on the wrestling ground.

He was emerging from the brothel when the litter bearing the young officer's body, carried by two infantrymen, passed by. About it, a detachment of cavalry was milling. The riders began to dismount. Septimus strode toward them. He knew the young officer. Everyone on the post did. They respected and feared him and knew that he was destined for high rank.

'What happened to him?' he asked a cavalryman who had just swung out of his saddle.

'He went out alone. The Jews ambushed him.'

Septimus shook his head slowly. 'Well,' he said, 'we have prisoners, you know. It will not go easy with them. I can personally promise you that.'

'Good!' said the soldier. 'Let their screams of agony be heard through every part of the city.'

Septimus rubbed his great paws together and was silent. He

did not have to speak; his hands would speak plainly enough for him when the time came. His giant feet stirred on the earth. He watched the litter pass slowly across the yard and disappear into a building. Then he said, 'Will he live?'

'If he does not,' said the soldier, 'then every Jew in this city will not.'

FIFTY-THREE

The sun threw broad shafts of light down from the sky and the desert flamed deep orange. Hills, clumps of cactus, infrequent terebinths and acacias threw lengthening shadows. In the dry waddies, shadow collected like water. Sky had softened; earth responded.

They rode southward. The stallion moved at his own pace over the firm earth littered with volcanic rock. Though they had been travelling for hours without a stop, Jesus sat erect. The girl sat behind him, clasping him loosely about the waist and sometimes leaning her head against his back. Though she looked weary, her eyes were luminous and shone with deep satisfaction.

'When one is a child,' Jesus said, 'he is a stranger in a world of adults whose words and deeds seem to have terrible consequences and everlasting meaning. But as one grows older, the giants keep shrinking. Their words are for the most part foolish and their actions fade.

'Yet do the adults delude themselves. They persuade themselves, and try to persuade others, that they will be on this earth forever; that their achievements will be remembered eternally. They are so terrified of their mortality and the fact that they will disappear that they invent an opposite myth. He who is honest and truly grows from childhood looks about him and sees that most have not grown: they are yet as infants, begging for some womb of paradise. They are still infants in the sense that they believe in giants. Only now they believe that they themselves are the giants. And they believe that they always were giants; that they never had an infancy or a childhood. For this would make them whole and mortal.

'Because,' Jesus continued, 'the world of infancy and childhood is a world of profound emotion. If men could but recognize their childhood, accept their emotion and honestly face their mortality, how much better it would be for them. If the world can become a dream again, somewhat in the way it was when men were children, through such acceptance, how much happier men would be.

'It is a cruel paradox that the very preoccupation with immortality destroys it: the more one is concerned with ending the rule of time, the more tyrannically it reigns. In a sense, to give up the lie of immortality is to gain the truth of it: that only the moment dissolved is immortal.

'I say to you,' Jesus went on, 'that there is no overall transcendental meaning to our lives. But there is a transcendental meaning of each man's life, though it is transcendental to him and to him alone. If men would only learn to see life as a dream, and therefore take it less 'seriously', as is indeed the case with their dreams, life would instantly take on a seriousness it had lost since childhood.

'How can this come about? Who will teach this to men? I do not know. I cannot answer. What I do know is that things are distorted by men, that they are wrenched out of proportion, that the balance of life has been lost. Men seize upon a fragment of life and try to call it the whole. Men are afraid of fear that must be, far more afraid of the idea that they fear than of what they fear. Men are terrified of admitting that at times they are helpless, which they are. Men are ashamed of their tenderness and compassion and deny them until, in the end, they lose them and become lesser men. Ultimately, they become mere objects driven by their own fear of self-discovery and self-acceptance.

'For most men,' said Jesus, 'do not have the capacity to truly accept what they are. They have disclaimed it, rejected it, and surrendered it. They hate themselves and what they do accept is that hatred. They fear any 'weakness' in themselves and so choose to defend themselves from this fear by acquiring 'power'. How sad and ironic that a man must defend himself against the terrible thought that he might be weak and mortal through an insatiable lust for power. The man who does this is, indeed, powerless: he is powerless to halt his illusory pursuit; and at the end, his power comes to nothing.

'Is not the world a reflection of the self-immolatory lust of a madman? Do not hatred and greed rule it? Does not the soldier's boot, the tyrant's whip, the lecher's claw, hold sway on this earth?'

Jesus paused. The wind had died completely and the air was clear. The sun's rays grew thick like the sediment of wine. The girl pressed close to him and hugged him and he spoke again.

'They wanted me to be a magician, but neither I nor any man in this world can be that. And I will not pretend to be what I am not, no matter how much they wanted me to pretend so that they, in turn, could pretend. I cannot wave a wand and change a man's body; neither can I transform his heart. Each man in this life must struggle with his own body and his own heart. Each must seek an answer from himself and with that answer question life and wait for a reply. Yes, wait. For there is that which time alone has to tell. Time will answer with the timelessness of birth and death.'

They had been riding a hill and as Jesus finished speaking they reached its crest. On the downward slope, a terrible sight met their eyes. Men, women, and children were scattered over the hillside in grotesque attitudes of death. Some of the bodies had been completely hacked to pieces and flung about. Entrails, gore, splinters of skull, blood, and hair were strewn to the very bottom of the decline, where jackals and vultures were gorging themselves.

The girl screamed and the horse reared back. Jesus calmed it, dismounted, and helped the girl down. Half-fainting, she fell into his arms and he caressed and comforted her. But she continued to sob and then, falling to her knees, vomited. Jesus held her forehead and wiped her mouth.

'I feel better,' she eventually murmured.

'Good,' said Jesus.

They both stood silently on the hill and gazed down at the carnage, which was raked by the bloody comb of the sun.

'What happened?' whispered the girl.

'The Roman cavalry found them.'

'Who . . . who were they?'

'Men, women, children. Humans like us.'

'What did they do?'

'They tried to find some answers,' said Jesus. 'Like us.'

'But why?' implored the girl. 'Why did the Romans slaughter them?'

'I don't know. Perhaps because they were afraid.'

'The people?'

'No, the Romans.'

A dreadful stink rose from the dead flesh. Light bubbled out of the sinking sun as if out of a slashed throat. Through the sky came new flights of buzzards, tumbling slowly across space. The girl trembled and began to weep once more. Her shoulders shook convulsively.

'Stay where you are,' said Jesus. 'I'll be right back.'

He started down the slope, stepping over the mangled corpses which lay among the puncture tracks of horses' hooves struck sharply into the dirt. An eyeless face stared up at him. Another face had its jaw slashed away. A third had no skull. The dead hands of a mother reached out for her infant, which lay dead in another place, its mouth frozen on a cry for her. There was no sign of life anywhere, except for the scavengers who were too bloated and confident to care about the intruder. Just as he was turning to retrace his steps, a stir caught his eye. He hurried over to the body and knelt by it.

The man was still alive. He was the hulking mute, the prophet who had led the band of beggars and cripples away from Jerusalem and into the desert, the man who had promised them salvation. His hair, face, neck, and arms were spattered with blood and slime. Jesus gazed into his living eyes and bent forward. 'What is it?' he said. 'What do you want to say? What do you want to tell me? Speak. I am not afraid to listen.'

The man's trembling lips moved. His tongue wagged. But no words came out. Jesus understood.

FIFTY-FOUR

The stone-faced bodyservant helped Pontius Pilate with his imperial robe of justice and as soon as he slipped into it, he felt better, more adequate, and safe in this vestment, a symbol of the power and order of civilization. He smiled wanly at the officer of protocol and the chief of the Imperial Court Guard and these functionaries returned his smile tenfold, bowing their heads slightly before his august presence. Generously, he suffered the valet to brush a few invisible specks of dirt from the severe folds of the heavy garment with its scarlet-and-gold trimming. He abruptly turned away, not at all surprising the servants who knew well his habits. Pilate squared his shoulders, froze the features of his distinguished face, and passed through the high archway into the court chamber proper. He looked neither right nor left. The others followed at a respectful distance.

A tall bailiff stood rigidly at attention and bawled out, in a shattering bass, 'His Excellency, the Procurator of Judea! All hail Pontius Pilate!'

The court chamber guards, clad in scarlet and silver, lined the walls of the room. At the rear of the hall, behind a latticework partition, ragged spectators bowed their heads. Pilate did not acknowledge the salute in any way. He approached the Great Chair of Judgment, which was set on a marble dais, and, carefully lifting the skirts of the robe, settled himself on his throne.

He gazed out somberly over the enormous hall. Two columns of thick marble pillars ran down its centre and its windows were set far up in the great walls. Light fanned down in cold waves, seeming to assert the lofty judgmental powers of the imperial court and the lowliness of those who stood before it accused. In the centre of the ceiling's dome, a skylight was set. If they chose, spectators and prisoners alike could look up at it and be reminded by the living eye of chilly light that the same equanimous luminescence burned in the heart of the judge, representative and instrument of Roman justice. Directly beneath the skylight, in a wooden pen, were the accused men. Two of them stood. The third, crippled by blows received from his captors, huddled on the floor.

The Procurator of Judea was comfortable. Guarded by the geometrically perfect rows of court guards, flanked on every side by court officials, aides, scribes and messengers, and reassured by the flawless symmetry of the chamber itself, he felt at ease, even expansive. The trial was certain to run smoothly. He sighed and raised the signet ring finger. The officer of protocol took heed and made a signal to the prosecutor to begin.

Short and slight, with a crooked shoulder and a leathery, worn face which was deceptive in that its lines of wear implied understanding and compassion, the prosecutor stepped forward to the lip of the dais, bowed from the waist, and addressed the man in the chair. 'Your Excellency, the case that is before you today is simple and clear-cut. There are no subtleties, no exigencies, no extenuating cirucumstances connected to it. It is a direct matter of a brutal assault by Jewish criminals on a routine patrol of the army of Rome in Judea, an attack that cost the life of one of our valiant soldiers and, as I have been given to understand in the last few minutes, the all but fatal wounding of one of the flowers of our corps of officers. . . .'

Here, the prosecutor mentioned the name and rank of the young officer and there was a stir among the officials. The prosecutor cleared his throat. 'The accused,' he continued, 'who appear before Your Excellency and this court in their utter depravity and bestiality, were all three implicated in the initial attack of which I spoke. This took place shortly before dawn today near the Valley of Kidron. Two of the prisoners, the one on the right and the one on the floor, were members of the murderous gang. The one on the left gave the other two succour and shelter in his nearby home. On a lonely knoll, a Roman solider perished and his commanding officer narrowly escaped the assassins' swords.'

Growing somewhat restless, Pilate fidgeted on his seat. He frowned severely and said in an even tone, 'Was there a witness to this monstrous act?'

'There was, Your Excellency.'

'And is he in this court of justice at the present time to testify?'

'He is not, Your Excellency.'

'And why is he not?'

'Because, Your Excellency,' said the prosecutor, 'because at this very moment he lies at the door of death. That is the reason, Your Excellency.' A tremor ran through the prosecutor's voice. 'He is the very same officer who escaped the murderers' blades at dawn and who, in the name of sacred duty and in the love of service to the empire and the emperor, rode out alone and unaccompanied, to seek out, hunt down, and destroy the Jewish agitators and criminals who had taken a man from him.

'I regret to inform you, Your Excellency,' said the prosecutor, dropping his voice, 'that courageous and lion-hearted as he was, the officer was unsuccessful. The vipers set a snare for him and brought him low. Even as I speak these words to you and to this court, his noble life hangs by a mere thread.'

Pilate nodded gloomily. He loathed these tales of attack and retribution, of warfare and violence. They depressed him when he heard them and gave him bad dreams at night. What a devilish day this was turning out to be! If only that damned city commander had not pressured him, he should have postponed the trial! Now there were rebels, ambushes, blood, death, Jews. Everything was jiggling around again, tipping over. The small of his back ached. He felt the first pangs of indigestion. The prosecutor was staring fixedly at him. The eyes of all the court officials were on him. He squirmed and, laying a finger along his nose, said, 'Has the witness, this officer, been able to make the proper deposition against the accused prisoners?'

The prosecutor glanced over to the officer of protocol who, in turn, nodded and said in a ringing voice: 'Yes, he has, most honourable prosecutor. He made such a deposition before he was struck down and it is in the possession of the court.'

The prosecutor turned his eyes once again to the Procurator.

'We have the deposition, Your Excellency, as you have

heard. There is nothing lacking but punishment for the guilty parties.'

Pilate was silent. His discomfort had increased; his interest was waning. 'Have the accused anything to say for themselves?' he asked. 'If so, they may address this imperial court of Rome now.'

A hush fell over the great chamber.

The prosecutor, clasping his hands behind his back, coughed nervously and shuffled his feet. The chief of the court guards whispered to an adjutant. From on high, the metallic eye of the skylight stared impassively down.

FIFTY-FIVE

He saw the physicians bend over him. They hovered over him like ghosts, arching their eyebrows and probing his flesh with their fingers and instruments. Then they withdrew to confer.

After a time, the hollow-chested physician returned and leaned over him.

'Can you hear me?' he asked.

'I hear you.'

'Fine. I wish to inform you of our conclusions.'

'Speak.'

'Well, the other doctors and I have decided that we can do nothing more for you. We cannot help you.'

'I did not expect anything from the lot of you.'

The doctor's faced paled. 'We feel that there is only one man in the city of Jerusalem who may be able to help you. He is ... a great surgeon and healer of men.'

'Who is the man?'

'A Jewish doctor.'

'No,' said the young officer.

The physician shrugged. 'As you decide. We will not summon him, according to the wish you have expressed.'

'What will happen to me?' asked the young officer.

'You will die.'

'Are you certain of that?'

'No one can be certain. In our opinion, you will surely die.'

A wave of nausea from the pain came over the officer. He did not want a filthy Jew to touch him, but he did not want to die. There was no point in it. He saw the doctor turning to leave.

'Wait,' he said, fighting for each word. 'Wait a moment. I've changed my mind. Get the Jew....'

He fainted.

FIFTY-SIX

Jesus stretched forth his hands and held the mute's ruined face between them, but the lips ceased to move. Slowly, the light faded from his eyes and left two opaque discs. Jesus eased the head back to the earth and as he did so caught sight of a gaping wound at the base of the mute's skull. He rose, stared at the shuddering body for several seconds, and then began his way uphill through the field of corpses.

The girl waited for him. She threw her arms around his neck and kissed his face and lips. Then the two of them went silently to the horse, mounted it, and rode off to the southeast. There was a dazed look on Jesus' face. The girl clung to him and trembled.

'People,' said Jesus bitterly, after a time, 'would do better to concentrate on what is possible in this life and not wish for miracles, for what cannot be done. There is nothing anyone can do for those people on the hillside. But the Romans can be stopped.'

The girl did not reply. The sun sank lower, weary with the day, weary of its task. The desert oranges turned to browns. In the west, the sky flamed like a cauldron. To the east, its blue fell apart and great streaks of grey appeared like rifts in it. They had reached the edge of a vast decline at whose bottom, like a giant fingernail implanted in the flesh of the land, the Sea of Salt appeared. Jesus reined the stallion to a halt.

'We must leave the horse,' he said.

'Leave it?'

'Yes. We'll go on from here by foot. I don't want the horse to be found anywhere in the vicinity of the cave.'

'I understand.'

They dismounted. Jesus patted the neck and flank of the animal and then slapped its rump. The stallion trotted off, throwing its head and snorting. They watched him go until he was only a speck in the blaze of the western sky. Jesus took the girl's hand and they began the long, slow descent.

It was almost dark when they reached their destination. Soon, in another hour or so, stars like enormous white moths would hang tremblingly in the black desert sky. Jesus pointed to the cave, but the girl could not see its mouth. It was set high in the face of a cliff, its entrance concealed by a projecting shelf of rock. There was a secret path by which they reached it.

Panting and exhausted, covered with rock dust and sand from the climb, they crawled in. After they had caught their breath, Jesus disappeared into the cave's depths. He returned with a wicker basket. From it, he drew forth dried dates and figs, olives, hard cheese, and bread. He unsealed a jug which he had also brought and gave it to the girl to drink, though he cautioned her to drink sparingly. They both ate ravenously. Then they lay in each other's arms on the dry rock floor and slept as one.

FIFTY-SEVEN

The three prisoners did not stir in their wooden pen.

Simeon slept on the floor. He was in shock and did not see nor hear clearly what went on in the court chamber. Over and over in his hazy mind, scenes from his past life appeared, mingled with strange shapes out of dreams and fantasies. Words thrust themselves into his consciousness, but they flew around like bats and did not form sentences. Even the words, when he tried to examine them, changed shapes or broke apart. He was in pain. His head whirled. He felt obscurely that his life was slipping through his fingers and that he could do nothing to save it.

The idiot stood like a mummy on the right. His face was blank. His hands were clasped together at his chest, as if he were praying but somehow knew that nobody would listen to the prayers of an idiot. Jesus' cloak was wrapped about him like a shroud. From time to time, a tiny sound, like the timid cry of a field mouse, would slip from his mouth. But in the vastness of the court hall, it was always lost.

The master of the house, though terrified, was the most aware of the three men. He had enough presence of mind to know what was going on and to follow the proceedings, but he could not cope with the direction. Thoughts of his wife and children intruded into the troubled stream of his reasoning. Sometimes it seemed to him that they actually stood with him in the pen, pulling at his clothes, demanding his attention, begging him to come home with them. Two or three times he jerked his head about as if to speak to them.

His house, his fields, his grain in storage, and his livestock were in danger. What would happen to it all? What would happen to his family? Then he thought of another man courting his wife. He saw them lying together in his bed. He shuddered. Or perhaps the Romans would sack everything. Perhaps they would confiscate it all. He saw his wife and children turned out, begging, dying.

How had all of this happened to him? How had he been brought to this in one swift stroke? Over and over the events leading up to the *Seder* and the *Seder* itself went through his mind, as if he had been sentenced to some hideous torture. He saw the cunning face of Peter proposing the *Seder*. He saw Peter's stubby fingers paying him out, coin by coin, the sum they had agreed on. He recalled smiling and thinking what a good deal he had made and how much profit there would be, just for allowing a bunch of scatterbrained religious fanatics to hold their Passover service under his roof. He remembered the *Seder* itself. He had drunk to celebrate the financial coup he had pulled off. Why not? He had declared that all in the household might drink to their fill. Why not? It was not every night in the year or in one's life that one could be so merry.

Then there was something about the dog. He remembered it only blurrily with great shame. He heard its howl of agony. He saw blood squirting from its shredded muzzle, oozing from its eyesockets. What had happened? Who had done it? Had it been he? Why? He saw the hound lying dead near the fig tree. Why? He had no answer, only a deep sense of horror.

His mind returned to the court chamber. Dimly, as though he were a great distance away, he saw the figure of Pontius Pilate in the chair on the dais. To his eyes, the Procurator of Judea looked like a statue. How curious it was that the statue could speak and how incredible that its last few words had been addressed to the accused. The master of the house knew that he was among the accused. But he had done nothing wrong, had taken no step against the government, had sheltered no one in his home except for the poor idiot who could do little more than whimper and stumble about. Why was he then accused? Why then had they taken him prisoner and caged him in the court-room?

He realized suddenly that the lofty presence on the dais had, in his regal generosity, given him the chance to speak in his defence. Trembling, he took a step forward and grasped the wooden bars of the pen. He lifted his head and with a faltering tongue began to speak: 'Your Excellency, most exalted judge. . . .'

Pilate heard faint sounds from the prisoners' pen, but he could not make out what they were. He did not even deign to glance at the speaker. He stared gloomily at the prosecutor's scarred, grizzly face and then down at his own highly polished and manicured nails. Inwardly, he cursed the city commander and his military impertinence.

'Your Highness,' the master of the house went on, stammering, 'I am completely innocent of the charges brought against me. I have always been a good and a loyal citizen of this land and a faithful and obedient subject of Rome.' Tears welled up in his eyes. 'Your Excellency,' he suddenly blurted out, 'I do not want to die.' He burst into sobs.

From the dome above, the fading light of day fell blankly upon him and his cellmates.

FIFTY-EIGHT

Herod saw blood on the tile floor. Then he grimaced, and shut his eyes. Blind, he passed a hand over his face, his forehead, nose, cheeks, chin. He was yet Herod. He opened his eyes. Blood on the floor. They were killing again. The Jews and the Romans were at it once more, hacking each other to pieces. A bitter taste flooded his mouth. He felt sick. He felt impotent. He wished he were dead. He was frightened of the wish.

He looked again at the pool of blood. It wasn't blood at all – it was wine. How absurd! He burst out laughing and rolled over on his back. He marvelled to see that he was completely naked. How droll. A naked king.

Then he realized where he was and the strangeness of his nudity faded. Everyone else in the lavish chamber was naked as well. He had misread things. This had happened to him more and more often recently. Evil and innocence jumped about constantly in his head. He kept seeing things in reverse. He was no longer able to believe in the purity of any action: something opposed always lurked behind it and threatened to break through.

Somehow, and Herod could not explain it, an inner balance had been destroyed and he was compelled to wander in its ruins. He could not right matters. Although he did not believe in them, he sometimes felt that he was possessed by demons. There were time when faces and objects long familiar to him became unrecognizable. He often had premonitions of injury and death. He was drawn to do things which he knew there was no sense in doing. He repeated ritual words and phrases over and over. He was frequently overcome by melancholy whose origins he could not locate. When he caught sight of his image in a mirror, he was taken aback. He did not know who it was.

He rose up on an elbow and glanced around him. Naked bodies sprawled with limbs entwined on every bed, divan, couch, and rug in the room. Men and women lay together, man and man, woman and woman, trios, quartets, whole groups. They were all asleep or dead. Or perhaps their flesh was ghost flesh, a spectral circus of thighs, arms, buttocks, legs, breasts, necks, penises, backs, testicles, hands. Herod sniffed. A naked woman lay on either side of him. They reeked of perfume and stank of wine.

He was disgusted. They all might have been fish in an aquarium. He was spent. His head ached. His back and legs hurt. Nausea bubbled up his throat. He was afraid an apparition might appear. Maybe the wine would turn into blood, or the bodies of the exhausted revellers into cadavers? Wine and blood: were they not alike? Living man and corpse: did not but moments of breathing separate one from the other? He grew anxious. He hated to think such thoughts. He did not believe that his mind was made for them.

He sighed. He was utterly worn out. He needed a rest. He needed to be where nobody and nothing could disturb him. His mind suggested the grave; he was horrified by the thought. Why did he have to think it?

He sat up carefully so as not to waken either of the women. They were young girls, virgins who had been selected and tested for his exclusive pleasure. He had taken his pleasure with them, emptying himself into them until he was thoroughly dry. He could no longer look at them. He did not want to hear them speak. He had no use for them. Their youth sickened him. Their lives did not exist for him.

He lifted a hand and made a signal for a servant to attend him. He caught the eye of an old and trusted eunuch, who made his way cautiously across the room, helped Herod from the bed, and led him to the bath. Then he summoned another pair of attendants and together the three men bathed and massaged the king. Herod sighed with pleasure and groaned with relief. He nodded and from time to time glanced up at the deeply lined face of the eunuch with something remotely akin to interest. But the treatment revived him quickly and banished any interest. His head cleared, his anxiety abated, his hauteur returned. He rose from the massage table, allowed the servants to fit him with a clean robe, permitted them to dab him with scent, and went back into the chamber of revelry.

By this time, nearly all of the party goers were stirring. Some of them drew gowns or covers over themselves. Others headed for the bath, singly or in couples or groups. Still others began to drink again and dally with each other; they sported openly, unashamedly, swallowing all in their lust and in turn being swallowed. Herod squared his shoulders and sucked in his belly. The weariness was gone and with it the gloom. He felt as if he fitted into his own skin.

Smiling, he looked around for the master of the house, his gracious host and dear friend, Hyrkanos. It was difficult to spot him in the large room, now filled with moving figures who seemed to have been released suddenly from a spell of immobility. A servant, seeing him standing in the doorway and looking about, came over to offer him aid. Herod, with a characteristic snarl, roughly shoved the man away. He was alive and well and vigorous and required the help of no one!

Herod laughed. There was his friend, at last! He started across the room, keeping his eyes on Hrykanos, who, naked, crawled on all fours toward the very puddle of wine Herod had seen on waking. The master of this splendid house and fortune was a big man, with red hair and crowded constellations of rust-coloured freckles spread over his shoulders and back. As he crawled, his huge paunch swung beneath his frame like an udder. A servant moved toward the spilt wine as if to mop it up and Hyrkanos raised his craggy head and bellowed at him with such fury that the young eunuch fled in terror. Everyone roared with merriment. Herod called out, 'Splendid!'

Then a short, blonde-haired girl with large breasts and swollen purple nipples flung herself on Hyrkanos' back. She straddled him with her meaty thighs and legs, pummelling him with her fists and urging him on like a horse. Everyone clapped and shouted and Herod screamed, 'Wonderful! Wonderful!'

Hyrkanos, with the naked girl on his back, reached the wine. He bent his head and began to lap it up greedily. The girl pumped up and down astride him, squeezing with her thighs, rubbing with her buttocks. Beneath her, Hyrkanos kept lapping the wine. He grew red. His member began to stiffen and the circle of onlookers cheered.

From a nearby window, a flash of light hit Herod's eye.

Annoyed, he glanced away from the sport toward the window which faced the hill of Golgotha. The helmet of a soldier standing beneath a tall crucifix had caught a ray of the setting sun and disturbed the king. Muttering under his breath, Herod turned his attention to Hyrkanos and the girl. Both had collapsed to the floor and were rolling in the wine. Herod forced his way through the spectators, flung off his robe, and got down on all fours. He howled like a wolf and threw himself at the copulating pair.

FIFTY-NINE

His restored vision showed him the face of a man he had never before seen. It was a thin, pinched face, with small, keen eyes under full brows, a sensual mouth, and a beard shot through with grey. The young officer regarded it coldly. He felt pain, but it was nothing compared to the pain he had experienced previously. Best of all, he had a whole field of consciousness in which to manoeuvre. Wetting his lips, he said, 'Where are my doctors?'

'I am your doctor. How do you feel?'

'You are my doctor? Who are you?'

The other ignored his question. 'How are you feeling? Do you have pain in your spine? How are your legs?'

'I know,' said the young officer, 'you are the Jew.'

'I asked you whether you have sensation in your legs. I wish you would answer me properly.'

'It is none of your affair how I feel. I do not answer Jewish questions.'

The other was silent. His face grew dark. At length, he said, 'I see. You have no further need of me now that you are out of danger. That much is apparent. I will be going then. Further treatment will be administered by the post physicians. I will report to them in full on your condition.'

He turned to go but the young officer's voice held him. 'Nobody dismissed you.'

'Excuse me, I didn't quite understand what you said. . . .'

'I said that nobody gave you permission to leave, Jew. And see that you listen to me more carefully. I am not in the habit of repeating myself.'

'I am leaving now,' said the other.

He started away from the bed.

'I order you to halt where you are, Jew.'

The small, slightly stooped man continued across the room. The young officer's voice leaped out like a whip, 'Guard!'

The lone guard at the door responded instantly.

'Sir?'

'Arrest that man.'

'Arrest the . . . physician, sir?'

'Are you deaf, soldier? Or are you derelict in your duty? Which is it, fool?'

'Sir, I—'

'Carry out my order this minute or I will level an insubordination charge against you!'

The doctor suddenly felt weary, felt so old that he could not take another step. He had made a mistake; he knew that now, when it was too late. He had trodden on an asp and when he lifted the foot it struck. He sighed and looked at the soldier who barred his way. He was a pale youth with acne scars still on his cheeks. His eyes were watery blue and would not stare directly at the doctor. He was undoubtedly a new recruit, inexperienced, unsure of himself. There was still a chance.

'Let me pass,' the doctor said sternly.

The soldier did not move. He had drawn his sword. He wet his dry lips with his tongue, as he glanced nervously from the doctor to the officer's bed.

'Sir,' he began, but left off.

A great bitterness came over the doctor. In a clear, loud voice, he said, 'Let me pass, soldier. The patient is in a delirium and does not know what he is saying. Out of my way!'

He stretched out a thin arm and tried to push the youth aside, but the soldier held fast. The officer's voice said flatly, 'Kill him.'

'Sir?'

'Kill him!' screamed the officer. 'Strike him down with your sword for resisting arrest and flouting the commands of a Roman officer!'

The physician turned his head to look at the face of the man who had issued such an order. That was another mistake. Livid with rage at the sight of his enemy's face, the officer roared, 'Kill him, you swine, or I'll have your testicles cut off and flung to the jackals!'

And, shaking from head to toe and using all of his strength, the soldier struck at the bared patch of the physician's neck with his sword.

SIXTY

Pilate rose slowly from his chair, smoothing the folds of his judicial robe. He had pronounced the verdict of guilty that carried with it a mandatory sentence of death. The city commander and his whole infernal military machine would be satisfied and would leave him alone . . . until the next time.

As he left the court chamber, he put on his most grave face, glancing neither to the right nor the left. The officials, aides, messengers, and scribes bowed to him. He acknowledged none of their salutations. He was the very sober visage of justice, the stern but ever constant, ever dependable face of Roman civilization.

The courtroom was being cleared. The throng of spectators, who would now move on to the hill of Golgotha and the executions, jostled and pushed its way out. The court guards turned precisely in their perfect files and began to mark time until they could march forward. From the prisoners' pen came the faint sounds made only by the master of the house, all that his sobs had become. They could have been made by a bird in a cage for the attention they attracted. In a short time, the pen was unlocked and the accused half-dragged and half-carried out a special exit to a wagon waiting to transport them to the hill of skulls. At last, the great chamber emptied out. Silence returned. The skylight, darkening, looked down impassively on the figure of one man who had not departed. He was the prosecutor. Hands clasped behind his back, he stood in a trance. There was a wry expression on his wizened face, as if he were loathe to leave.

At home, Pilate retired at once to his veranda and stretched himself out on a divan. He yawned and did not trouble himself to cover his mouth. A servant brought him a glass of chilled wine. He sipped it slowly, and stared out over the walls of his palace toward the empurpled hills over which the sky was banked like a furnace. The heat of the day had ebbed; a coolness was setting in; the haunting scent of spring filled the clear air. The night would be cool, with stars like newly minted coins flung over the velvet of the heavens.

Pilate sighed deeply. This could have been such a pleasant land. It was true that its landscapes were at times too stark, but it was nevertheless an attractive country. It was even, on occasion, strangely moving, with a beauty all its own, a beauty he had encountered nowhere else. If only the Jews who populated it were not forever stirring up trouble, forever rebelling, forever chasing phantoms! He closed his eyes. He preferred not thinking about how it might have been because that immediately brought to mind the way things were.

The wine did help. It was good. It tingled on his palate and mounted to his head. He began to relax. The morning's cares faded; the courtroom dissolved. If the city commander had walked in on him now unexpectedly, he should have greeted him with a smile. He held out his goblet, and out of the gathering darkness a servant came forward and filled it to the brim.

He let memories of bygone days wash into his mind and even allowed himself to dream a little. Why not? This was a splendid twilight hour in a splendid day. The last torches of daylight were smouldering in the sky, soon to be extinguished. An expectant hush was in the air. The willows in the garden stirred slightly. Was this not the finest hour he had? His heart expanded. Why could not men live this way in peace and tranquillity?

Soft footsteps approached him. He inclined his head and heard what his chief manservant whispered in his ear. He smiled and nodded. The servant withdrew. A few moments later, a young maidservant appeared on the veranda. Pilate beckoned to her and she went over to the divan. She wore only the thinnest of garments over her plump body. Still sipping his wine, Pilate plucked at it with his free hand.

SIXTY-ONE

Jesus dreamed that he was flying.

He was high over the earth, high over his earth, Judea. His arms were outstretched like the wings of a bird. Below, very small and black, his shadow glided over the desert. It looked like a cross.

He flew to the outskirts of Jerusalem, not far from the Gate of the Essenes. A dreadful sight met his eyes. A great red pall spewed forth from the city. Clouds of smoke billowed upward from its houses and towers. Jesus was still aloft, but he seemed to have lost some of the power of his flight. Intense waves of heat rolled out at him, and he was compelled to retreat. Suddenly, he could hear the screams of men and women, the wailing of infants and the terrified sounds of animals.

Walls collapsed before his eyes, groaning as they began to go and howling as they crumbled into debris. It seemed to Jesus that the gates of the city were shut up and locked and that none could go forth from it. In vain he tried to get closer. The awful heat did not permit him to pass through. Finally, desperately, he cried out for mercy. There was no answer, but the savage crackling of flames, the rain of ashes whirled about by the wind, and the towering clouds of smoke that rose stubbornly into the sky.

Jesus then caught sight of Peter and the other disciples. They were clear of the city, walking along the road that led south into the desert. It was a long time since Jesus had seen them. They looked indolent and withdrawn. When had they left the city? How had they managed to get out when nobody else could? Why were they leaving? Why didn't they try to help? Jesus swooped down and landed before them on their way.

Excepting Peter, who seemed somehow to have expected him, the disciples were astonished and taken aback. Several began to run away before Peter stopped them with a snarl.

Then, when he was satisfied they would not flee, he turned to Jesus and glared. 'Why have you come back to us?' he said.

'Jerusalem is burning,' said Jesus. 'Don't you see?'

'Let it burn.'

'Did you come from inside the city? Is there a way out? A secret passage? A hidden route of escape?'

'Why do you want to know?'

'Can we save anyone?' pleaded Jesus.

'Save?' Peter laughed bitterly. 'Of course! Oh, certainly! Save whom you want to save, Jesus. Or save whom you can, I should say. . . .'

'You haven't answered my questions.'

'I don't have to answer your questions. Not at all! Neither do you have the right to question us. We are not happy to see you. Leave us. Go your own way and don't plague us. You are a bad omen to us, you and that girl of yours.'

'What do you know about the girl? Have you seen her? Where is she?'

'Know about your slut?' leered Peter. 'Well, for one thing, I know she's in the city. And for another, I know she'll be burned to a cinder with the rest of them. How does that suit you?'

Jesus cried out and would have struck Peter in the face, but the other disciples pressed so closely around him and hemmed him in so tightly that he could not raise a hand. Their faces, ringing him so closely, seemed all at once to be alike and blank, lit by the red glare from the inferno Jerusalem had become. Jesus was powerless, and Peter sensed it and laughed loudly, a fierce, cruel laugh that stung Jesus' ears.

And then the faces of the disciples turned to skulls and Jesus realized that Peter was the grinning skull of death itself, and that he was claiming Jerusalem. And Jesus cried out bitterly and wept sorely.

SIXTY-TWO

Peter saw the riderless horse come toward him, and he read in the event a sign of providence. Providence had also sent along a Roman cavalry saddle which was a certain death warrant should he be found with it. He therefore pulled it from the stallion's back, cursing under his breath as he did so, as if to conceal the curse from providence, and flung it to the ground. Then he mounted the animal and set off in the direction of Jerusalem.

After an hour of riding, he was covered with a paste of dust and sweat and his eyes were bloodshot. Brown sand stuck to their lashes and to his lips. He looked like the first man God had ever modelled from the earth. But he was tired of lonely earth, fed up with ascetic life, and weary of his plans to convert men and transform the world. Instead, he would change himself. As he rode, he worked out his ideas.

He would rend his clothes, cast off his sandals, and enter Jerusalem as a beggar. Even if Jesus had talked, had told everything there was to tell, they would never be able to recognize him as the Peter they sought. Even if the authorities were to catch him in a dragnet, he would affect epilepsy and fall into a trance when they tried to question him. He knew how to roll his eyes and foam at the mouth. They would get nothing from him but the ravings of a madman. They would know nothing, while he, behind his mask, would be watching their every move, reckoning and plotting a new way and a new life.

In the new life, he would have power and authority. He would direct men and decide their end: some to live and some to die. He would be feared and respected. All would bow low to him. Women would adulate and adore him. He would capture the hearts and imagination of royalty. He would receive the undying loyalty of warriors and princes. He would be a king.

The sun set, fiery and inscrutable. It cut across the tableland of the desert with its last, chastened scimitars of flame. It depressed Peter. Everything depressed him. He hated himself and he hated life. He hated the grit in his mouth, the aching in his calves, the monotonous rhythm of the stallion's hooves, the thirst in his breast, the hunger in his belly, the stale fantasies which crept into his mind. He prodded the horse to greater speed. It tossed its head, but obeyed. In the end, he thought, when he had real power, life would obey him.

Jerusalem, when he first caught sight of it in the red light of the sun, seemed to be on fire. He ground his teeth. He wanted to set it on fire, so great was his anger against the race of man. No man knew him for the titan he was. No man saw the power that was within him: none dreamed that this beggar, clad in rags and covered with the dust of the desert, was a monarch and would one day rule over hosts. Again, he cursed under his breath. This time no man could hear him.

When he felt he had come close enough to the walls of the city, he climbed down from the horse and kicked it. Peter shaded his eyes and peered ahead as the horse vanished from sight at a gallop. He observed a large mob moving toward the stony hill of Golgotha. Some strong instinct told him there were executions in the wind. Peter had a nose for death; he was seldom wrong about it.

Quickly, he moved up to the crowd and slipped into it. He furtively shifted his eyes to see if he had been noticed. He had not. He was relieved. He felt lost and safe in the jostling and shuffling of the throng. All around him, his neighbours panted and wheezed and choked on the bitter dust of the path. Their eyes bugged; their fingers twitched at their throats and clawed at their chests; their shoulders hunched. They kept going as their feet moved step after step, unstopping and unfaltering.

Peter breathed easily. His look was to the hill of skulls, Golgotha. He saw what he knew he would see: crosses glistening in the last light of the dying sun.

SIXTY-THREE

Peter and the disciples disappeared at once.

Jesus was alone before the burning city and he beheld it in terror and grief. A wave of utter and complete helplessness came over him and he fell upon his knees.

'My God,' he cried out brokenly, 'why is there such suffering in this world? For whose sake? To what purpose? Why are we living creatures so lost? What can I do?'

Except for the crackling and hissing of the flames, punctuated frequently by the collapse of a building or a battlement, there was no sound of reply. The screams and shrieks of the inhabitants had ceased.

Jesus continued to kneel. After a time he heard a voice, though he could determine neither where it came from nor what it said. Then Jesus saw a serpent and he knew that the voice had come forth from its mouth. He recognized the voice as that of Peter.

'*I thought you were gone,*' *said Jesus.*

The serpent's next words were intelligible. '*I am never gone.*'

'*I know you,*' *said Jesus.* '*You cannot disguise yourself. You may have the form of a viper, but you are Peter.*'

The serpent laughed. '*I am you.*'

Jesus' wrath waxed hot as he rose up and snatched a stick from the ground and struck out at the snake. It eluded his blows each time, laughing as it slid away.

'*You cannot touch me,*' *it hissed.* '*Try as you may, you will never strike me. You will smite only my shadow.*'

Jesus sprang from side to side, thrashing the earth with his stick, but could not reach the viper. The serpent skidded away, coiling and hissing. Its voice rose to so terrible a pitch that Jesus had to stop up his ears. When he uncovered them again, all was silence. He gazed back at the city. The flames had gone;

the fire was out. Jerusalem was a mound of ashes, a heap of grey slag.

Then the serpent appeared before Jesus' eyes once more, halting between him and the dead city. It was only a pale shadow on the earth, though its voice was clear.

'Do you wish to see the girl again?' it said.

'She lives?' cried Jesus. 'Where?'

'Do you want to see her?'

'You have not told me yet if she lives, evil one. I do not wish to see her dead.'

'She lives.'

'Where is she?'

'I will take you there. Follow me.'

No living thing stirred in the city. Over its rubble, a dark pall of ash hung. Jesus went around its blackened wall. In the distance, he caught sight of Golgotha, the hill of skulls. He shrank back, but the serpent admonished him. 'If you want to see the girl, you must follow me.'

'Are you certain she lives? Or do you lie?'

'She is alive.'

'How do I know you tell me the truth?'

'You have no choice but to trust me.'

At the foot of the hill of skulls, which lay like a gigantic rock in the backwash of blasted light from the charred ruins of the city, Jesus felt he could go no further. He had seen the shadows of the three crucifixes bent down over the brow of the hill. He faltered and stopped in his tracks. The serpent chided him, urged him on, threatened him, and spoke ill of the girl. Jesus' knees sagged, and his body buckled to the ground. He lay there on his stomach and shook until the viper, on its belly as well, said coldly, 'This is the last time I will speak to you. If you want to see the girl alive, you must get on your feet and come with me.'

Then Jesus struggled to his feet and ascended the hill where the crosses stood. There were three, one for each shadow: to the right and the left, they were empty. On the centre one, the girl had been impaled. She was naked. The blood still oozed from her wounds. Jesus gazed up at her and she looked down at him, her eyes shining with anguish, her lips parted to speak the

149

words of love and recognition she could not utter. Jesus stretched out his arms to her.

Now he knew that indeed the viper had not lied to him; the girl was alive. He dropped his arms and glanced around the crest of the hill out of the corner of his eyes, hoping to take the viper unaware. He wanted to slay it, but it was gone, though its presence hovered in the cindery air. Then Jesus heard its loathsome voice for the last time.

'And the two empty crosses that stand at her sides? Do you wonder, Jesus, what they are for? I will make it clear to you. One is for your sorrow, Jesus. And the other is for your helplessness.

SIXTY-FOUR

The slaughtered body of the Jewish physician was pulled from the room, dragged across the yard, and flung onto the dung heap. The floor was scrubbed spotless by two orderlies who had been commanded to remove every trace of Jewish blood from it. The youthful guard, who had become ill and vomited after the slaying, was replaced by a squat, red-necked bulldog of a soldier who had been through numerous campaigns. Later the young officer was borne on a litter from the room where the physicians had attended him to the sick bay. He squinted in the failing daylight, but made no sound as he was moved from one point to another.

Only one other patient lay in the sick bay. He was a cavalryman who had been bitten while out on patrol by a poisonous snake. He cried out in his delirium. The young officer summoned an orderly and demanded that the cavalryman be taken out.

'But he's too ill to be moved, sir.'

'Get him out at once!'

Without another word they removed the sick man, and the officer was alone. His body was weak, but his anger burned with even greater intensity. No amount of spilt blood could sate it. Lying on his back, he watched the flies crawl sluggishly over the ceiling. From time to time, he glanced over at the window through which he could see a richly hued purple bougainvillea vine climbing over its latticework frame. For the first time since morning, he thought of the girl. Feature by feature, he reconstructed her face in his mind. Then he destroyed it with a blow of an imaginary mailed fist. Then he tried to envision the man who had been with her. He was vague about the man's body and about his face, but he saw the eyes clearly. He remembered the look in them as he had charged the couple on the stallion and he remembered their look when the man stood over him with a rock in his hand. His lips twisted. Those eyes would be gouged out and fed to a starving hound. That hand, and the rest of that body, would be bent to a lingering death on some crucifix outside the city walls. A Jewish jackal, when he died, ought to attract his fellow jackals with the stench of his rotting flesh!

He closed his eyes, certain that the couple would be caught and executed. Footsteps on the tiles roused him. A thin, wiry man with a quick, unmistakable step came toward him. It was the military commander of the city of Jerusalem. The young officer froze.

'At ease,' said the commander.

The young officer forced himself to relax as he had been ordered. He looked up into the face of his superior. It was a thin, bony face in keeping with the man's body. The lips were mere lines; the nose was so thin it brought to mind the edge of a knife blade; the chin was almost inconsequential. Over the skull, the hair was kinky and coiled tightly, shot through with grey and receding from the protuberant bone of the forehead, Of all his features, the eyes were most striking. They were set in narrow, deep sockets, and from them looks shot out like forked tongues or fixed on a man with terrible fastness.

'Am I disturbing you?'

'Not at all, sir. It is an honour.'

'How do you feel?'

'Fine, sir. Well. I should be up and at my duties in a short time, sir.'

'I have no doubt about that.'

The commander fell silent. The young officer met his gaze without flinching. He expected that his superior would question him about all that had transpired. But when the commander broke the silence at length, he said, 'Tell me, what manner of man are you?'

'Sir?'

'I mean to say, what is at the root of you?'

The young officer answered soberly, 'It would not be easy for me to tell you, sir. But then, if the commander will not consider my remark offensive or presumptuous, I do not think that it is really necessary for me to tell you. I think that you already know, sir.'

The city commander was not affronted; he was pleased. The young officer was absolutely correct. Looking down into those cold, blue-grey eyes, which steadfastly refused to enter into the caves of his own and be destroyed, he realized that he was looking into a mirror and viewed death.

SIXTY-FIVE

Septimus wore a close-fitting black garment which encased his giant's body. The cloak was held at the waist by a wide silver belt from which hung a dagger in a silver sheath. He had been known to use the knife once when a prisoner wrenched loose in an all but superhuman frenzy. The guards moved in on the man but were slow. The executioner had cut him to ribbons before their swords were properly drawn. In the hood worn over his head, there were slits for his eyes but no vent for the mouth. Septimus did not need to use his tongue; his hands spoke well enough for him.

He now stood impassively on Golgotha. His arms were folded across his massive chest, and his eyes were trained on the winding road that led up to the hill. A huge cloud of dust, ruddy with the rays of the sinking sun, churned over it. He knew that it was made by the mob which followed the cart in whose wooden cage the condemned prisoners lay in their own excrement.

The officer in charge of the death squad leaned against the centre crucifix and spat. 'I've never seen them slower than today. Something ought to be done about it, I tell you, it's a shame.

Septimus did not even glance at the officer. His attention was riveted toward the road, toward the ox-drawn cart which crept forward at such a rate that it scarcely seemed to move. He was not really concerned with its speed. He knew it would arrive and that he would be ready for it when it did. There was no hurry or rush at all.

Garbed in black, on the hill of skulls, Septimus the executioner was a lord of eternity. With his own two mortal hands, he passed men from this shore of the living over to the other one. The condemned men shrank back. They fell unconscious at his feet. They defecated. They wept and howled and pleaded because they did not desire to leave this shore and go on to that other. He had to help them along with his gargantuan strength. It was foolish to struggle. The journey was a simple one. All a man had to do was put himself in the executioner's hands. Nothing else was required.

Septimus smiled, but the black hood hid the smile. His hood hid every expression from those about to die. His face was blank, an enigma to them. Except for the light that glittered from his eye slits, it was not a human face; it was a mask that covered his humanity and perhaps absorbed it altogether. Perhaps, indeed, the gleam in the eyes of the executioner was only a reflection of the light that raced about in the prisoners' eyes like a trapped animal.

The death squad commander squirmed. He shook his head. An ugly look came over his face. 'I'm going to put in for a transfer,' he said. 'I'm going to get the hell out of this lousy unit. It bores me. I'm going to get myself another job.'

Septimus held up a hand to indicate silence. He needed silence so that he could concentrate his full energy on what lay ahead, so that he could commit himself wholly to the executions. Death was a jealous overseer and tolerated no distractions. For the man who executed, the process was a ritual. It began with the first notice, continued through the preparations and this last, long watch over the progress of the wagon and its attendant cavalcade, and terminated in the crucifixions themselves. Septimus ignored no minute detail. He valued each of them and seemed to absorb them all and draw from them a kind of cumulative charge. When the time came for him to do his job, he would clap his great paw on the prisoner's shoulder with absolute certainty. 'Here now,' he seemed to say in the force and finality of his grip, 'The hour for you to meet with death has come and I am the very man to give you a proper introduction to him. Don't worry about a thing. I know him well.'

On the ground, at the foot of the central crucifix, the tools of execution were stacked neatly: the rope that did not break, the long spikes that slipped with ease through flesh, the well-balanced hammer that drove them in. Septimus' eyes fell on them and his strength seemed to increase a hundredfold. He was huge; he was inescapable; he was a tower of death over the land.

SIXTY-SIX

The girl cried out, and Jesus wakened from his dream of her death. Overjoyed to find her alive, he embraced her and kissed her hair and face and lips.

'What's the matter?' he said softly.

At first, she wept and could not answer. After a time, she calmed down and spoke.

'I had a terrible dream,' she said, drawing closer to him. 'I dreamed you were caught by the Romans and put on trial and sentenced to death. They took you to a terrible hill outside the city walls, and nailed you to a cross. I stood in the crowd and watched it all. And when it was over, and the mob had departed, I drew near unto you and fell at the foot of your cross. I knelt on the earth that was wet with your blood. I cried.

'And the Roman soldiers drove me away. And then, suddenly, I was transformed into a dog and came up the hill to lie again at your feet. But then the soldiers approached me, shouting and cursing, and when I fled their kicks, one of them hurled a lance at me and it struck me and I fell. I lay wounded in the mud, while you looked down on me from the cross. You were unable to speak for your mouth was filled with the black blood of despair. And then the light in your eyes went out. I had nothing in the world; I was alone.

'Then the Roman soldiers mocked me and spat on me and abused me in my anguish. I wished to die and called out for death to come and take me. It did not come; I pleaded again. And then your corpse spoke to me from the crucifix, saying, "I am death." I cried out, "If you are death, come to me." And you answered, "I will come, my darling, but you must be patient." But I could not bear the thought of waiting for you when you were so near, and I cried, "If you will not come to me now, then you betray me!" And then I wakened.'

Jesus was silent. He sadly stroked her body and said, 'Once born, everything we do is a contradiction. This is because, already, with the very first breath we draw, we are dead. But, then, birth is itself a contradiction. In dreams, our contradictions are mirrored.'

'I am awake now, am I not?'

'You are awake.'

'What are we going to do, my darling?'

'I don't know yet,' said Jesus. 'We'll have to stay here for a while. The Romans will be scouring the countryside for victims. But they'll never find us in here. Unless one knows about it, the cave is invisible from below. And we have enough provisions to last us for at least a month. We're safe enough here.'

'Safe? On this earth?' The girl laughed bitterly.

'This earth is all we have. And the Romans will be gone one day.'

'The Romans will go, of course. And then others will come. There will always be Romans.'

'Perhaps not,' said Jesus.

They were silent for some time as they lay in each other's arms. Then the girl whispered, 'Would you . . . do you want . . . to have children?'

'I don't know,' he replied. 'I haven't really thought about it at all. Do you?'

'Of course I do. But I fear for children in this world.'

'We were children once,' said Jesus.

SIXTY-SEVEN

One eye was battered shut, but there was yet sight in the other; through it Simeon saw the city of Jerusalem in which he had spent most of his life. It did not look like Jerusalem, the city of his birth. In the light of the setting sun, it seemed to be ablaze, to be altogether unfamiliar to him, to be a place he had never before seen and would never see again.

Below him, too, the sight was strange. A great crowd had gathered. It was kept from coming closer to him by a squad of helmeted, black-plumed soldiers. This, too, was entirely unfamiliar to him, meant nothing to him, though he himself had many times, during the course of his life, been part of a crowd on this very hill and gazed up curiously at the human carrion on the wooden crosses.

Dimly, he realized that he was suspended between earth and sky, somehow fixed motionless between them. But he did not know how. He was plunged into an ocean of pain so vast that he could no longer say what caused it. His wounds festered. The blood oozed slowly from them. His lips were swollen and black. His body, nailed to its cross, had twisted itself into a monstrous shape, a perversion of the form of a man. Ripped to shreds, his clothes were caked with slime and excrement. Though his heart still beat, its beats were numbered. It was as if there were a line drawn beyond which his life could not go.

From his mind, too, the life ebbed. It stretched, cold and grey, like a barren desert plain. Every once in a while, a thought blew across it like a dry tumbleweed. Then only shreds of thoughts were left. Images flared and went out. A face, a figure, a place, a shape: all ran together and blurred. Yet in the cobweb they formed, he seemed to feel, in some deep layer of consciousness he had never before known or suspected, that a final shape was being worked out. There was a final shape which might explain all that troubled him, that had always troubled him. He desperately wanted to see it and to understand it.

When his lips parted and revealed teeth shattered into gums, he moaned. It was this terrible desire he was trying to express. He never got to see it. His breath flowed with difficulty through his nostrils. The sight of his open eye darkened until it saw no more than the other. At last his weary, mourning heart stopped beating, as if the final, invisible nail, driven by the hand and hammer of the executioner of all men, had been sunk into it.

SIXTY-EIGHT

Peter had never been present at an execution, and he found a curious excitement had come over him. He shivered and felt hot and cold spasms run over him when soldiers of the infamous Roman death squad, loathed and feared by the populace and even by other Roman soldiers, flung open the stout door of the wagon cage and dragged the condemned men from it.

Then it happened; he saw the sight that made his blood run cold. The third man to be pulled from the pen was Jesus! Peter could not see his face clearly because he was at the extreme edge of the crowd and the light was bad, but he knew the familiar shape of that skull, and he recognized beyond all doubt the cloak in which Jesus was wrapped. He had good reason to recognize it, for it was he who had given it to Jesus as a gift not more than three months ago when life was different, and he still entertained hopes for the man. Who, even three short weeks ago, would have dreamed of this grotesque end?

His teeth chattered and his breath came in painful gasps as Peter watched the executioner, a monster of a fellow wearing black garb and hooded in black. The members of the death squad moved expertly and swiftly about their business until three bodies were silhouetted, each on its cross of wood, against the bloody throat of the evening sky. Peter had felt fear and revulsion, but more than these he felt fascinated. He took his eyes from the spectacle long enough to glance about and see if he were being watched.

The man on the centre cross, between the other two, one of whom Peter had at length recognized as the master of the house in which they had held the *Seder*, was Jesus. Peter knew his body well. It had been graceful, slender, noble even. Now it looked like an insect, hideously mangled. Peter hated the new deformity, much – as he now realized – as he had hated the living man. He hoped Jesus had not talked. If he had, it did not matter. He was invisible to Rome and would remain so until things quieted down. He also knew that Rome would spill other blood and be satisfied. After all, it did not really matter to the Romans precisely whose blood it was as long as it flowed.

Calmer, Peter gave himself more fully to the details of the crucifixion and its aftermath. He wondered who would be the first of the three to die? Would it be Jesus? How long would he last? Would it be possible to fix the exact instant of death? Would there be some unmistakable sign? Peter longed to know. He felt himself drawn to those three lives on their crucifixes, lives that hung between earth and heaven, lives that tottered on the brink of the void and must soon plunge headlong into it and disappear for all time. So great was his absorption that he forgot to keep watch. Hurriedly, he looked around. A chill of terror gripped his heart. To his right, separated from him by an old man, the glittering eyes of a woman were fastened on him. He tried to avert his glance, to twist his features to a look of idiocy, but found he could not. Something in the woman's stare held him fast. Something he was afraid to name. Despite his fear, he returned the look. A thrill of excitation ran through him.

SIXTY-NINE

The master of the house kept fainting.

He wanted to stop himself, because he realized that every faint brought him closer to death, that each temporary darkness was a claim upon him by final darkness. He tried to check himself, but each time a coldness came over him: it began as a hard knot of nausea in the pit of his stomach and rose in an icy wave to engulf his mind. He found himself on the edge of a pit and could not keep himself from toppling into it. Each time he regained consciousness, he swore that he would hold onto it. But his will meant nothing. A stronger will prevailed.

When he was awake, he felt himself awake in a way that he had never before known. He seemed to see more clearly, to see in a new manner, to look into the heart of things. Each object in the landscape, every face in the crowd was revealed to him not only in its minutest detail but in a fresh light. It was as if, for the first time in his life, he had the power to understand what things really were and what they intended in the world. And it seemed that now, at last, he could look into himself and understand why he had been born. It was not possible for him to say in so many words what the purpose of his life was, but he knew that he understood it perfectly and that knowledge filled him with elation. If only he were able to prevent himself from passing out, if only he could hold on to what he had.

Then the darkness came. He felt it come, saw it rise up before his eyes like a tidal wave and wash over him, filling his nose and mouth until he drowned in it. It pulled him down. He did not wish to go down. He struggled with all his might, but his strength was a mockery in the face of this invisible strength. Darkness possessed him: he lost all.

Then, suddenly, again without his willing it, he was awake once more. He saw the hill, Golgotha, the city, the crowd, the rays of the sun like raw scars on the sky. Joy flooded over him. It was as if he had been reborn. It was as if he had returned from fearsome death to greet the living world yet another time. So great was the sensation of the new birth that he could forget he was on his cross. His vision was without limit; he was king, seer, angel. He was a man who had been lowered into his grave and revived. He gazed raptly at the crowd, distinguished every face, read the look in every eye, fathomed the secret of every beating heart. If only his tongue could tell them what he knew.

Again he fainted and again he wakened. Again he sank and again he rose. Again he died and again he lived. Sweat crawled over his grimy face, which was losing its roundness and taking on a leanness. From his wounds, which had bled profusely when first they were inflicted, the blood dripped slowly, tirelessly. He felt pain but he no longer connected it with his own flesh: it seemed to be a part of the world.

The master of the house smiled. He smiled down at the crowd, at each breathing face in it. He even smiled at the members of the death squad in their black tunics and at the executioner in his hood. They had, he now knew, done nothing to him. They could do nothing to him. For he had met with death and bested it. They could not kill him because he could not die.

Even after the last shudder of life had departed from his crucified body, the smile stayed frozen on his face.

SEVENTY

As the sun died, the young officer's fever rose. He tossed fitfully on his cot and twice roused the orderly who sat beside him. When water was brought to him he refused it and sank into a delirium, groaning and lashing out with his hands. The orderly became alarmed and summoned a doctor, who shook his head after examining him. 'I don't know if he will live through the night,' he said. 'Complications have set in and I am not equipped to deal with them. The only man who could have treated him is dead.'

The orderly bowed respectfully and the physician left. Rubbing his eyes and yawning, the orderly seated himself again beside his charge and dozed off almost immediately.

The sick man twisted and moaned on his cot. In his delirium, he saw himself on the field of battle. It was a level plain, littered as far as the eye could see with the skulls and bones of warriors. It appeared that he alone of all the combatants had remained alive. But he was sorely puzzled. The bones of the dead had been picked clean by scavengers months or perhaps years ago. Yet he still stood on the field, fresh, in full battle array, shield strapped to forearm, sword drawn for action. How was he there so long after the war had been fought? Why was his sword in his hand ready for the kill? Where was the adversary?

He had the feeling that some obscure danger lurked about, that some menace he could not see threatened him. Nothing stirred; nothing moved. On the flat, grey plain that stretched to the horizon in every direction were scattered the dry warped bones of fallen soldiers. One could no longer say in which army they had fought.

He began to walk. His feet moved quickly, surely. He kept his sword at the ready. Occasionally, he kicked aside a rib or shard of skull. Nothing changed as he walked. The landscape stayed the same. The bones were the same. It was as if he had never left the spot from which he started. Nor was there a sign that the day moved on. The sky was overcast, as grey as the earth he trod. And as he went on, he noticed that he cast no shadow. Then a voice spoke to him and he whirled, his sword sweeping in a wide circle: he could not discover from where the voice came.

'Fool!' the voice called out. 'Do you wonder not that you cast no shadow?'

'I cast no shadow because there is no sun above my head,' said the young officer, searching for some sign of the speaker.

'Now,' said the voice, 'now there is sun and still you cast no shadow.'

And there was sun: a blazing ball of sun in a stark sky. And the officer saw that he stood beneath it and yet there appeared no shadow of his body on the earth.

'Fool! Do you still fail to understand? Are you still unable to solve the riddle?'

'Who calls a Roman officer a fool dies a swift and terrible death!'

But the voice laughed. And the young officer suddenly saw a black shadow, his own shadow, on the earth before him. And then the shadow sprang up from the ground and confronted him with its shadow sword, the exact counterpart of his. And the voice laughed and spoke again, saying, 'Roman officer! Fool! Your shadow is your adversary!'

SEVENTY-ONE

As soon as she set eyes on Peter, she knew he was no beggar. True, he was clad in beggar's rags, but she saw immediately that this was a disguise. As well, she sensed that he was in the crowd for the same reasons as she. Her curiosity became aroused and her sensuality inflamed as she viewed him. His face was swarthy, heavy-fleshed, and very sensual with a lumpy, large-nostrilled nose and eyelids like lead weights.

Her attention began to shift from the men on the crucifixes, who had by this time lost some of their original charm. The giant, hooded executioner, of whom she had often heard but never seen, had performed with a skill that had almost made her swoon. His work now completed, he had quit the hill of Golgotha like a gargantuan bird of prey which had sated itself and would fly away for a well-earned sleep. Behind him, he left his handiwork on the three crosses. The men of the death squad remained swarming around like insects, forever restless, forever fretting, forever licking the boot soles of the angel of extermination.

As her interest in the dying prisoners waned, she turned her head to observe the mob. Her eyes roamed it idly until they reached Peter. A fierce thrill, a hungry shudder, ran through her. She saw how he kept glancing around. She knew immediately that he feared detection. Here, too, she thought, was an executioner, but different from the one who had presided over the ceremonies on Golgotha. Here was a man who was cunning and devious and adroit at concealing his cruelty. Here was lust and carefully hidden rage, destructiveness and moral deformity. She shivered again and bit her lip until blood spurted from it.

When he caught sight of her, he turned away as if he had been touched by fire. Her breath came hard. She had to get to him, to touch him, to taste his corruption.

At that moment a cry rang out from one of the crosses, a cry almost like that of a bird in a treetop. It was impossible to say from which crucifix it came. There was no movement from any of them and the light had failed. The crowd was startled and all eyes once again looked to the execution. But there was nothing more than the single utterance, dislodged like a stone from a cliff of silence and swallowed as abruptly as it had come. There were only the blackening stonelike bodies.

She looked again for him in order to seek him out, but he had changed his position in the instant she had shifted her eyes to the crucifixion. She was furious, outraged. Had she not been incognito and without accompanying servants and guards, she would have commanded the crowd to be scoured for him. She would have shaken him out of his protective mob as an insect is shaken out of a rug. She wanted him. She was frantic. She began to push and shove her way through the throng, which was already breaking up. Her eyes blazed. She felt stifled in the cloak she had thrown about her. Her body itched as if vermin were upon her. She gasped for breath. It would be impossible to locate him in the melee and growing darkness. She wanted to howl with despair.

But then, just as she had abandoned hope and was about to make her way back to the palace and return to her role as Herod's wife, she found him. She had bumped into him and did not see his face. But his mouth was close to hers and she recognized him by the odour of putrefaction.

SEVENTY-TWO

Only one was still alive. He had not spoken a single word since the time he was arrested, nor did he utter one during the time of his crucifixion. His bruised lips parted, but the sound of his agony did not come forth. Froth filled his mouth and spilled onto his chin and neck. His eyes rolled upward, revealing their whites. The cloak that Jesus had given him was befouled and torn.

Throughout all, he was limp, unprotesting, mute. He remained silent as the executioner, four times his size, went about his work, assisted by two members of the death squad whose help was not needed. He went up easily and hung lightly, even gagging without sound. The experts expected that he would be the first to go.

They were wrong; he was the last. Though life had fled the bodies of the two men who flanked him, it still pulsed through his slight frame. The others had died and he still lived. The executioner was gone and still he lived. The crowd dispersed and still he lived. The sun was departed and night came and the stars bubbled soundlessly into the sky and still he did not die. He hung, alive, on his cross.

The soldiers of the death squad were confounded. How was it that this idiot lived on when the other two had already dropped away? They had been bigger and hardier than he and yet they were gone before him. They vanished and he lasted. How could you account for that? Did the idiot feel less pain? Did his blood flow less readily? Was his heart stouter? Were his nerves better? Did he possess some secret charm? Was witchcraft involved? How could one know?

Below his scrawny feet, the soldiers gathered and argued. They made wagers on when he would go. One man doubted that he was really alive. To prove it, he reached up with his sword and pricked the sole of a foot. The body twitched and the doubting soldier was mocked. The man who lived, as they began to call him, became the only topic of conversation. He became a joke. They laughed and shouted hoarse obscenities at him. He became an obsession. They cursed him and spat up at him. Every little while, somebody else stuck a sword and dagger in him to make certain he still lived. When his flesh told them he did, they pushed each other and clapped each other's shoulders and giggled nervously and began to be afraid. They could not remember a man who lasted so long. They began casting worried glances up at him. The pricks stopped. It was unnatural and they almost expected some dreadful thing to happen, something they feared to name even in their thoughts.

They were wrong; nothing happened. His body hung lightly, like a shell, as it had from the start. His flesh was limp; it did not move. It did not utter unearthly cries. It did not burst into flame. No angel descended nor demon ascended to snatch it. It was simply alive on the cross, one arm stretched toward the city of Jerusalem, the other toward the hills that surrounded it, and it continued to live. They could not understand why.

SEVENTY-THREE

The cave seemed to Jesus to be a womb at the very centre of the
earth, where nothing evil could happen, and he fell into a deep,
untroubled sleep. Something wakened him. He listened tensely
and sensed that the girl was awake beside him, listening too.

There! He had not been wrong. He heard the noise again. It
came from toward the mouth of the cave. Cautiously, he put out
a hand to reach for a rock. But the girl clutched his shoulder.
She handed him her knife. He took it and leaned forward,
straining to hear.

Now there was a continuous, scraping sound. A rock fell
outside the cave and then a second went. They rattled down the
precipice and dirt hissed after them. Something was there, and
it did not sound like an animal. Jesus was puzzled. The cave
was difficult to discover by daylight, and impossible to find by
nightfall. It was highly unlikely that a Roman patrol would
come this far after dark. Jesus gripped the knife. He had never
used one against a man, but he had no doubt that he would.

Someone was in the cave. He had seen the figure of a man
silhouetted for an instant against the cave's opening. He could
no longer wait. 'Who's there?'

Silence. Jesus could not make the man out. 'Who has entered
my cave?'

A voice answered him in Hebrew: 'Who says this is your
cave?'

'I say it is mine,' Jesus answered.

'By what right?' said the intruder.

'I have lived here for many years. My sect occupied many
caves in this area. But who are you to question me this way?
Why did you enter my home?'

In perfect Jerusalemite Hebrew, the man told Jesus that he
was a Zealot and that the name he gave was a code name.

'Is it all right?' whispered the girl. 'He is not a Roman, is
he?'

'It's all right,' said Jesus. 'He is who he says he is.'

'We thought this cave to be unoccupied,' said the Zealot. 'We've seen no one about it for many months. I, myself, have been within it several times during the past few weeks and found no sign of occupancy. But we have disturbed nothing.'

'I've been away,' said Jesus, 'with the members of my sect.'

'And now you've returned?'

'Yes and no.'

'What do you mean?'

'I've not returned to the sect. Just to the cave with my wife.'

'Are you in hiding?'

'Yes.'

'I see,' said the Zealot. Then he said, 'Did you hear about the executions scheduled in Jerusalem this past evening? Three men were to be crucified on Golgotha for armed rebellion against the authorities.'

'Who were they? Why were they charged with rebellion?'

'Why? Does it matter why? The Romans charge people with whatever jumps into their heads. They think that by destroying the flesh of some, they can kill the spirit of others, but we have very different ideas.'

'What are your ideas?' asked Jesus.

'Resistance,' said the Zealot. 'That's why I'm here in this cave. We wanted to use it and the others around here. . . .'

'Use them?'

'Yes. As bases for attacks on the Romans. And as hide-outs.'

'You and your comrades plan to wage war on the Romans?'

'Exactly,' said the Zealot. 'We have it in our minds to teach them this lesson: that death is a whore and can be induced to visit any mortal on this earth, even the oppressor.'

SEVENTY-FOUR

The standing shadow vanished and he glanced up at the sky to see if the sun were still there, but the sun had turned into a gigantic skull. Though he was awed, the young officer was not dismayed. His lips curled with disdain. 'Where is my adversary?' he cried out. 'What have you done with my shadow?'

The skull sun opened its gruesome maw and grinned. Each of its yellowed, broken teeth was as large as a mountain. In its vast eyesockets, thousands of buzzards roosted. Gripping his sword firmly, the young officer lifted his head even higher and shouted, 'Do you think I am afraid? Do you think that an officer of Rome will cower before you? Is that it? Well, you are wrong. I am ready to meet you as I am. You will never make me afraid. Do with me what you will!'

But the grinning skull vanished from the sky without a sound. Before him now, floating bodiless in the air, was the face of the girl he had desired to possess and then desired to kill. She was pale; her hair was dishevelled. Her eyes had a haunted look in them, a look that roused murderous anger in him. Raising his weapon, he took a step towards it, but it rose high above his reach and then continued to rise in the sky.

He followed its progress, but it grew brighter as it ascended. He was blinded. Its dazzling reflection danced in his brain and made him dizzy. He covered his face and staggered about until at last the vertigo passed away, and he was able to open his eyes and see once more.

He saw at once that his shadow had returned and lay at his feet on the earth. It was very black and sharply defined. He stared at it, ready for any move it might make against him. Then the voice spoke to him, saying, 'Officer of Rome. Flower of the corps. You say that you fear no man. Do you then fear a woman?'

'I fear no one,' cried the young officer.

And from his shadow came the laugh of a woman. And from

the middle of the shadow there appeared a red wound, and from it blood began to ooze. The young officer was paralyzed. He did not know what to think or do. The orb face in the sky threw down a terrible heat. He dared not look at it again. His flesh was covered with sweat. His chest and throat ached with thirst. Spots flew before his eyes.

In a sudden fit of rage, he bent and thrust the sword at the shadow. Instantly, it was pulled from his fingers by a force more powerful than he had ever known. He stood and saw it disappear into the bleeding wound before he had time to reach out for it. He put his hands to his temples. How could a wound swallow a weapon?

Then the shadow woman's voice spoke to him, saying, 'So shall you and all your hosts be swallowed!'

Faint with thirst and groggy with the heat, the young officer dropped on one knee to the earth. He hung his head, hating himself for the weakness which had overcome him. He glanced down and saw that the blood from the shadow had reached his knee. He struggled to rise. Instead, his other knee came down. The flow of thick blood engulfed him. The heat grew even more intense. He felt he must die of thirst. Then the shadow woman's voice whispered to him, 'Drink ...'

'No.'

'Drink ...'

'Never.'

'But you will drink.'

But in the end he bent far forward and knelt on all fours like a beast of the field and drank the warm, stinking blood of the woman's wound. He gagged and he retched. He vomited back into the fibrous fluid and he bent and drank the blood with his own vomit.

'This is a dream,' he told himself in horror. 'It is not real.'

He did not believe what he said.

SEVENTY-FIVE

The constellations reeled in the sky and still he did not die. Quarrels broke out among the soldiers of the death squad, who were on edge. Their commander threatened severe punishment. His second-in-command, a lean, slope-shouldered, balding man who had fallen from a position of grace in a legion headquarters unit because of sexual indiscretion, said to him in a hoarse whisper, 'You know, I can actually hear him breathing on the cross.'

'It's impossible to hear him breathing! It's your demented mind playing tricks on you again! Next you'll be telling me that you're back at the headquarters unit, where everyone kissed your behind, again!'

'There's really no need for that kind of sarcasm, you know.'

'No need for it? You don't say. Well, maybe there's no need for you around here, either. But what can I do about it, eh? To whom can I complain?' The commander nodded to the crucifix in the centre. 'To him up there?'

'Don't joke about it,' shuddered the second-in-command. 'It's nothing to jest about, I tell you. Don't these infernal Jews ever die? Do they last forever? It's absolutely inhuman, I say. And it's plaguing the life out of the men. I've never seen anything like this in my life.'

'Why do you always have to rub it in, damn your scrofulous hide!'

'I'm not rubbing it in' – the second-in-command stroked his chin nervously – 'I just think that we ought to do something about it, that's all.'

'And what would you suggest?' said the commander.

The other looked around furtively and then said, 'We could call the executioner, couldn't we?'

'Imbecile! The executioner's been here already!'

'I know, I know he's been here. But . . . but—'

'But what?'

The second-in-command fidgeted; he looked like a great, awkward stork. 'But, well, you know.' He glanced up at the centre cross and lowered his voice. 'This man doesn't seem to want to die. He doesn't seem to have to die.'

The commander of the death squad said nothing. He followed the gaze of his subordinate up to where the idiot hung on the crucifix, backed by the immensity of the night sky and its drunken luminaries. The man who lived was quiet and uncomplaining. He seemed to be free. One easily imagined his body floating in space, tethered neither to heaven nor earth. One could imagine it taking off and soaring up into the starry night, where perhaps it belonged. The commander had seen many men executed, but he had never seen one die so unprotestingly. Nor had he ever seen a man stay alive on the cross for so long a time.

Though he could and would not reveal his feelings to his second-in-command and his men, he too was worried and unnerved. He would, indeed, have liked to summon the monster in the hood so that it would all end. By law, nobody else was permitted to touch a condemned man. But how could he call the executioner in the early hours of the morning? It had never happened before. There was no precedent. What if the fellow died before Septimus arrived? He would be a laughingstock. The unit would be ridiculed. He might even be relieved of his command and his second put above him. He pulled himself together, gave his subordinate a withering look of contempt, and said, 'Ignoramus! Of course he has to die. Everyone has to die. And they will. And so will he.'

'But when?'

'When it is time for him to die.'

'But when is that?'

'Only death knows,' said the commander.

And he cleared his throat and spat at the centre cross. He was terrified of spitting at the man nailed to it.

SEVENTY-SIX

The movement of the crowd had thrown the two of them together. As soon as their bodies touched, they knew there could be no mistake. She caught Peter's arm as if to tell him he would not get away from her again. She had no reason to worry, for he no longer had any desire to escape. He understood what her body said; his own body burned.

Still, she whispered, 'Why are you here? Why did you come to this place?'

'For the same reason as you,' he said.

'What reason is that?'

She thrust her loins against his. His face grew dark. The blood coursed painfully through his body. They struggled in the crowd, their flesh grew feverish and began to ache for release. Finally, they got to the edge of the mob and broke loose. Peter was panting. She had a rash of fine sweat above her upper lip. They held to each other with greedy fingers.

'This way,' she said.

Slipping and stumbling, they moved around the side of the hill of skulls, until they were behind the three crosses. The bodies on them were barely discernible blurs. Below, the hill ended in a declivity filled with tall weeds. Often, the corpses of the executed were flung there if nobody claimed them. Sometimes, the carcasses of stray dogs or cats or jackals killed for sport by the soldiers were pitched down. The two of them scraped down the slope and plunged headlong into the weeds. Peter's face was bloated purple with desire. Her lips hung open, showing feral teeth and a tongue like a bloodclot. He seized her. She screamed. He tore at her cloak and skirts. She scratched and bit him. Locked in each other's arms, they fell to the ground. Soon they copulated among the bones of the dead and the excrement of the living.

PART THREE

SEVENTY-SEVEN

The sun rose, bloody and immaculate.

And he rose from the dead. Yes, he had been dead and now he lived again. To any man in this world who confronted him, he could say: 'Yes, I have seen the land of the dead with mine own eyes and have come away to tell the tale. I was not affrighted by it; neither did I flee from it; neither was I vanquished by it. For am I not here before you to tell you this tale?'

His fever was gone. He felt fine. The young officer knew he would rise from his bed, and he would ride and fight and kill once more. He was satisfied. Death was another enemy, one of the many a man encountered on the earth. And it was a cowardly enemy who would attack a man only when he was ill and weak.

He lay quietly, savouring to the full the health and strength that was seeping slowly back into his limbs. Memories of past conflict came to mind. He saw himself girding for battle. He saw himself deal a crushing blow. He saw himself administer a coup de grace. He saw himself at the head of a charge. The faces of his victims blurred. They ran together to form a slough of mire, which he walked through, scraping his boots clean on a stone when he was out of it. On the other hand, his face grew brighter, even celestial. He felt himself invincible. There was not a foe he could not defeat.

He thought about the visit of the city commander. He tried to recall even the smallest detail. Everything about it seemed important, not to be overlooked. It was an augury of good. He sensed that he would rise high in the military hierarchy he served so well and so devotedly. It was almost as if the awesome power he so desired was already in his grasp.

He saw the magnificent array of a full legion in parade formation. Its armour and its weapons glittered brilliantly in the sun. Its standards fluttered in the air. Its trumpets blared the sounds of jubilation and victory. He was mounted on a match-less stallion. A cluster of aides sat on splendid steeds behind him. He reviewed the troops with a cold, unerring eye that froze the blood of the men in the ranks as they passed.

His concern had faded for the girl, her Jew lover, Jannaeus, the horse that had spilled him. What were they but inconsequential worms which one stepped on and crushed without a thought? His power seemed real to him, more real than anything in life. It was so real that he had no life outside it. With it, there was nothing in the world he was unable to destroy.

Suddenly, he thought he heard something. What? A voice? Dimly, deep within him, the voice of his dream, the voice of the shadow woman suggested itself, struggled to come into consciousness. But all that came through was a single, isolated spasm in his cheek. He heard nothing of the voice. He never had. He never would.

Sunlight flooded the room. A fly buzzed lazily. He watched it for a time, thinking nothing, and then, turning his head, noticed that the orderly beside him was sound asleep in his chair. The young officer promptly summoned the guard and had the man wakened roughly and arrested. He would be charged with dereliction of duty, tried, and sentenced to penal servitude. The army of Rome would be well rid of his kind.

SEVENTY-EIGHT

The sun rose, bloody and immaculate.

He died. He would not have died yet, he would have lived, his life would have gone on through the Jerusalem sunrise and beyond it into the new day had not the commander of the death squad succumbed to the unbearable tension. In a sudden fury, he had summoned the most brutish of his men and ordered him to cut the idiot's throat.

The deed was done instantly at the break of day. The brute stood on the shoulders of two of his comrades, while a third gripped his thick calves and supported him from the rear. Pushing back the crucified man's head with one hand, the soldier slashed his throat from ear to ear in one stroke. He did it well, hitting the jugular on the very first try. The blood spurted forth, soaking him and raining down on the men below. They cried out in disgust, jerked back, and almost dropped their burden. The brute wavered, clawed the air for balance, nearly fell and then at the last second sprang down safely. The bloody knife was in his hand. Even the commander and his second were spattered with drops of blood, but they tolerated it because they saw that the job had been accomplished. The men of the unit were sworn to secrecy; none would ever tell how the matter was finished.

Now, they stood and stared up at the centre cross, waiting for the end to come. The idiot's face was white. Blood gushed from his open throat and covered the entire front of his cloak. His eyes were wide open. They were very large and beautiful and they shone in the light of the morning like two giant drops of dew.

The man on the cross grew weaker. The body, which had learned so well to live on the cross, was losing its last strength. It could not learn to live with a cut throat. Every breath was a farewell to the life around it. A deep rattle began in his chest. His eyes, luminous as the stars that had kept company with him all the night long, filled with his last look at the earth. They stared out and it was as if they pulled everything, the whole world, the whole universe into them. Then they went out and were like two stones. His body stretched without grace on the crucifix.

The commander of the death squad sighed with relief. It was over at last. Looking haggard, even corpselike, as if his body were in secret sympathy with the three cadavers above his head, the second-in-command blew his nose noisily and muttered, 'I'm glad it's done and finished with. For a while I thought it would never end.'

'Everything ends,' said his superior. And then, glancing around nervously, he added, 'Except the Roman empire.'

SEVENTY-NINE

The sun rose, bloody and immaculate.

The two of them awoke at the same time, as if one obscene thought had jolted through their minds. Even in sleep, the lust was brewing and it boiled over as soon as they caught sight of each other. They embraced and kissed. Tonguing each other's mouth, they rolled over to couple once more in the weeds. Groaning and grunting on the soiled earth, each probed for the limit of vileness in the other and did not find it. Above their sweating bodies hung the shaken stalks of nettles and the curses of the soldiers on Golgotha.

They spent furtively, selfishly, even at the moment of greatest pleasure wanting to give nothing to each other, wanting only to hoard, to use, to lend as usurers. Like lizards, they blinked in the sunlight and lazily unlocked their loins. They were greedy with thoughts of their next pleasure and they were weary, as if even this early in the morning the life had been drained out of them. They were both surfeited, yet they starved for something they could not name.

Herod's wife suggested to Peter that he come with her to the court and live there. She would make a place for him as a retainer. Licking his lips, he readily agreed. They were well satisfied with the bargain they had struck; each thought he had the best of it. They rose, brushed themselves off, and stumbled forward through the weeds. When they glanced up, they saw the crucified men on top of the hill.

'Who are they?' she said. 'Do you know any of them?'

'Jewish dogs,' Peter said.

He kept looking at the centre cross. The body looked shriveled. Peter averted his eyes and spat.

'What's the matter?' she said.

'Nothing.'

'Can't you stand the sight of death?'

'I can stand it.'

'Then why did you shudder?'

'I did not shudder,' said Peter.

The woman laughed. 'You did. Of course you did. I saw you with my own eyes. Are you afraid?'

'I am not afraid.'

'Are you hiding something?'

'I am hiding nothing. I have nothing to hide.'

'Are you quite certain?' she sneered. 'Perhaps you are a murderer yourself?'

'What a stupid thing to say!'

'You think it's stupid; I don't. Perhaps you should be hanging from a cross?'

With all his might Peter slapped her across the face and a thrill went through both of them. Wiping the blood from her mouth, she smiled and said, 'Perhaps I should be hanging from one, eh?'

Peter did not answer her. They emerged from the nettles and began to move slowly up the hill. Despite himself, Peter looked over his shoulder at the three crosses. Soon they came upon a soldier of the death squad. He was squatting by a bush at stool. His tunic was bloodstained; even his face and hands were spattered with it. He was sweating and the flies buzzed thickly about his head and arms and thighs. He reeked of blood and feces.

'Are they all dead?' asked Peter, jerking his head up at the crucifixes.

The soldier grunted. 'They're all gone.'

'Are you sure?'

'They couldn't be deader,' panted the soldier, and sighed gratefully as a turd slipped out of him.

EIGHTY

The sun woke, bloody and immaculate.

And Jesus rose and beheld in the light streaming in from the mouth of the cave the form of the girl. She was still asleep. He sat beside her and looked at her closed eyes, her cheeks, her lips. His gaze lingered on her features. Through her garment, he saw the shape of her body and thought of her naked. He remembered the subtle beauty and mysterious perfection of her woman's figure. And when she wakened and smiled, he bent over her and kissed her mouth and she put her arms about his neck and drew him down to her. And they knew each other in the freshness and first light of the morning.

And when they were rested and had eaten the morning repast, they sat together and Jesus spoke, saying, 'What is this life we have been given without being asked if we desire it? Is it a dream?'

And the girl said, 'It is what we make of it before we sleep once more the great slumber that was before we were born.'

'Life,' said Jesus, 'runs through our fingers like the sand of the shore. What can we show for our lives? How can we say that we possess them? For even as we speak of our lives, they are fading in the sight of the earth. Even as we boast of our invulnerability and proclaim our deeds, the earth is taken from beneath our feet, grain by grain. We pretend that we are as rock, that we stand firm in the face of the tide, but we are eaten away as weed by the current of time. No, it is rather the flow of eternity that takes us. We have tried to tame and vanquish eternity by calling it time. Minute by minute, we are swept out to sea.

'The past is a graveyard and so is the future.'

'But each day,' said the girl, 'our lives rise from the grave and call out to us. They cry out to us to live.'

'Men,' Jesus said, 'desire immunity. But there is no immunity to life. They cry out to religion as to a saviour. It is in vain.

Religion can be nothing but love and compassion and the strength that comes from these. All else in religion is but smoke and bitter ash. The saviour is in each man as he acts to save his life.'

'And as for us,' said the girl, touching his face. 'Will we have a child? Have you thought about it?'

'We will have a child,' answered Jesus softly.

'And where shall we live? And how? Shall we remain in this cave, hidden from the world?'

And Jesus shook his head and said, 'I do not yet know. But I remember the words of the Zealot who came to us in the night. The word resistance is not forgotten. We shall see.'

'We shall see,' said the girl.

EIGHTY-ONE

The sun swelled, bloody and immaculate.

Judas yawned, brushed a fly away from his face without opening his eyes, and stretched his arms. He was not ready to wake up, but he sensed he would not sleep again. He was hungry and if he wanted to steal one of the chickens he had to do it right away, before the farm folk got up. He rubbed his eyes and opened them. Sunlight flooded over the earthen floor of the shed and sparkled over the straw on which he lay. Through the open doorway, he saw a goat sniffing at the dirt of the farmyard.

A sharp noise startled him and he turned his head. His heart sank. On the far side of the shed, where the cows were yoked, stood a tall, plump woman. At her feet was the milk pail she had flung purposely to the ground. She was staring directly at Judas and he rose on one elbow to a sitting position and began picking slivers of straw from his round, florid face. The dream of the chicken on the spit had fled. When the girl shouted for the farmhands to come, he would be lucky to escape without a good beating.

But the girl seated herself on a worn, wooden stool by the first cow, reached out a leg, and drew the pail to her with a bare foot, grasped two of the cow's teats in her large fingers, and began to milk. Judas watched her suspiciously until she suddenly looked up and smiled at him. She had a big, freckled, rotund face, much like Judas' face, large, even, white teeth and a huge bosom. Her hair was yellow, only a shade darker than the straw of the loft. As she milked, she kept smiling at Judas and never took her eyes from him. After a time, he decided to break the silence and said, 'Excuse me, but aren't you surprised to find me here?'

'No,' she replied.

'How's that?'

'I knew you were in the shed.'

'But how?'

'I was here an hour ago, fool. While you were asleep. You were so exhausted that you didn't waken when I came in. You didn't even wake up when I touched you.'

'Touched me? What do you mean?'

The milkmaid's eyes shone. She pushed an unruly lock of hair from her forehead. Her fingers abruptly stopped drawing milk from the udder into the pail wedged between her knees.

'You really don't know what I mean?'

'No.'

'You aren't jesting?'

'I am not.'

The girl's face grew more steadily red, as if some secret duct had opened beneath her smooth skin and was spreading scarlet dye. Carefully, she loosened the pressure of her legs on the pail and set it at a safe distance from the cow's legs. Then she pushed back the stool and rose. Her great bosom was lifting and falling rapidly. Brushing her skirts, she walked rapidly to the door of the shed, swung it closed, and fastened the latch from within.

An hour or so later, Judas lay on his back staring up at the golden shafts of sunlight that slipped through the cracks in the roof to the floor of straw-littered earth. The girl lay beside him with her skirts raised. The shed was a dim cavern. He could hear the cows chewing wetly and swishing their tails. Outside the locked door, the goat bleated.

'Well,' whispered the milkmaid, 'how did you like it?'

Judas swallowed hard. 'Do it again,' he said hoarsely.

Moaning, the girl rolled over and began once more.

EIGHTY-TWO

Three weeks later, a pleasure party which had ridden out of Herod's palace was on the road to Emmaus. The morning was bright, the sky almost without a cloud, trees were in full leaf, anemones and wild irises gleamed on the slopes of the hills, and vari-coloured butterflies sailed through the air.

The two riders in the lead were Herod's wife and her constant companion and paramour, Peter, whom she had installed at court. Their affair was the talk of aristocratic society and this pleased the two of them almost more than the affair itself. Mounted on sleek horses, they rode along slowly, chatting idly, enjoying the spring air and sunshine. They were in no particular hurry and had no special cares on their minds. They would stop eventually and lunch in the open.

A hundred yards ahead of them on the dusty road walked a couple: a young man and his woman. As the royal entourage came up to them, they stepped from the way into the field in order to let it pass. The two lead riders came abreast of them and Peter turned his head and glanced at them. He saw that the man was Jesus. Uttering a sharp cry, he fell unconscious from his horse.

When he came to, Herod's wife bent over him.

'What happened, you fool?' she said contemptuously. 'Did you see a ghost?'

He fainted again. And from that time he did not speak. He wandered about the palace in a daze for some weeks, scribbled incoherent notes which he often tore up before anyone could look at them, waved his arms wildly, recoiled at the sight of strangers, and fell into bouts of melancholy which bordered on stupor. Herod's wife had little patience. In the end, he was accounted a madman and sent into the streets of the city to beg silently for scraps. He died in a gutter without a word.

On the day Peter saw Jesus risen from the death he had wished him, they found the two bodies in the hovel at the end of the cul-de-sac. A terrible stink had come from the dwelling and the authorities finally investigated. Holding their noses and cursing, two officials entered the room and discovered the carcasses of man and dog, lying face to face on the earthen floor. The bloated corpses were black and swollen; their mouths were open and swarming with flies. It looked as if they were holding converse with each other in the language of the void.